NIGHTFLARE

Brendan Doms

To Ryan

— Brendan Doms

11/2016

Text and cover art copyright © 2016 Brendan Doms

Limited Edition Hardcover, 1st Printing

October 2016

ISBN: 978-0-9982197-0-7

Contents

This book is dedicated to all those who taught me, and continue to teach me, about language.

Without you, it'd be gibberish.

Part I
BOMB

Chapter 1: The Investigators

"Distracting." *Definitely the right word.*

"What?"

"It's distracting." *Confident. Be confident.*

"Well I think it's *disgusting*. And you're pale enough that I'm afraid you're going to lose it in your helmet."

The man turned his head away from the woman, away from the scene, and spoke again: "It's just distracting."

Frozen blood splattered two walls, a frosty corona for the mangled remains in the corner. The victuals had been perfectly preserved by the vacuum of space after being disbursed by the explosive decompression.

"This was a lab, obviously. Do we know what they were working on?" *Keep talking. Keep your mind on other things.*

"Beyond something biochemical in nature, I can't say."

"It could be a drug or vaccine."

"Could be a dirty bomb."

He gulped. "We'll have to impose quarantine then, as soon as we get out. Is there a forensics team coming?"

She chuckled, "We *are* the forensics team. And the data team. Turn-key detectives. Unprecedented doesn't even cover it. The suits and ties downstairs never expected a murder up here. We were just lucky enough to pull the shift when it happened."

"That's annoying, not lucky." He looked out at the vast expanse of stars visible through the strips of metal bending outward opposite the body, a human-sized hole exposing the whole room to space. He imagined a wild wind howling through the breach and felt an extreme sense of displacement, a state-of-being vertigo: here, the default was dead. Everything inanimate, except for him and his partner. And the only thing separating him from the unmoving collective was thin fabric, glass, and plastic, twisted together into a fragile suit that would eventually, effortlessly, suffocate him. His own breath had become a form of suicide. Breathe in. One less second to live.

Space was a raw deal for humans.

Nodding toward the breach, he framed his perceptions into a coherent question: "Could we have a potential survivor?"

Later, in hindsight, he realized she never even considered the question.

"Certainly not. Unless this was premeditated and whoever it was brought a spacesuit along. But it looks far too spur of the moment for that. If you actually looked at our crime scene instead of cringing away you'd have figured that out for yourself."

He glanced back at the gruesomeness again. Some anonymous man — a youth really, though barely recognizable as such — had a large chunk of his throat missing and deep finger-spaced gouges on the opposite shoulder. "Not exactly precision work."

"No. And I'd go so far to say that it was the decompression that actually killed him. Though the wounds would have given time. As for the attacker, we should ask the station for a priority sweep of any debris in the area that matches a person's mass."

"So there was some struggle. One punches through the wall while the other is gasping for breath. Doesn't really make sense. Is there surveillance?"

She shook her head. "I don't see a camera. If this is a private lab they won't record what goes on in here. Security and secrecy being paramount and all that. We'll have to do it the old-fashioned way. ID this sap and compare him with the employee records and see who else was on shift. Make sure to get some fingernail scrapes as evidence of the attacker.

Then we'll do some good old interrogation of everyone they knew and worked with."

"You make it sound so easy. But we've never dealt with anything remotely like this before."

"Maybe I'm overconfident, but the case seems pretty cut-and-dry."

"Well I, for one, have a bad feeling about this."

"By the pricking of my thumbs?"

"Precisely."

She focused on him then, eyes narrow, searching his being for a sign of power, of prescience. Finding nothing, she got back to work.

He looked over the interior of the small, plain cube. At the shattered vials twinkling reflected starlight. At the manufactured glove keeping his hand pressurized. At his partner in her spacesuit. Technologies that some time ago had been created in a lab not unlike this one. At the boy in the corner who could've been mauled by a giant wolf. And despite all the questions and unknowns, the uncertainties already plaguing the investigation of the very first murder in space, he already knew without any doubt: "This case is going to be very *distracting*."

Chapter 2: The Assistant and the Veteran

The Assistant leaned his side against the plastic bar. It was painted with a brown finish to make it appear like one of those classic mahogany bars planet-side, a poor imitation of a solid, reliable chunk of wood that would never get shipped up to a remote station. A bar like that would weigh far too much to be worth the fuel needed for it to escape Earth's gravity. No, this bar — which he trusted to support himself — was like all the other furniture on the station: cheap, light, and easy to clean. The Assistant downed the last of his refreshing yet tasteless beer and ordered a replacement when the Veteran entered and took the spot next to him.

The Veteran was an old, grizzled man. Naturally balding and perpetually sporting a five o'clock shadow, it wasn't widely known which of the past Earthly conflicts he had participated in — perhaps all of them — but few had the courage to ask. The Assistant typically only spoke to him when he had to.

"There's a mess in that lab you work in, boy." The Veteran hadn't ordered, and he wasn't looking directly at the Assistant. He was inspecting the top-shelf whiskeys while acting like he was reporting on the weather.

"Well I'm off today. I'm sure the Doc can handle it."

"You didn't hear me, boy. I just got back from detail on it."

There was a sudden jerk and the loud bass boom of a distant explosion as the bartender delivered the Assistant's next round. It remained untouched as he felt adrenaline overwhelm the alcohol in his blood.

"That would be the lab separating from the station then."

The Assistant was having trouble getting his tongue to work right. "Separating? But why?"

"Quarantine, of course. That old Doc of yours looks to have floated into space. Feds want to keep whatever you were working on away from the rest of us. And keep you from tampering with the evidence, I suspect."

Now the blood was rushing into his leg muscles — begging him to flee when his mind knew that running would only bring him full circle around the station after a dozen minutes. "So there are feds? And the Doc is missing?"

"Missing? Ain't you listening? Dead, boy! They have radar sweeping the vacuum for him right now. Seems that other one of you labs rats tossed the Doc through the wall when they had a scuffle."

The Assistant's brain stalled for a minute as he put the pieces together. The realization came slowly, dragging its feet from the depths of his conscience: "But if my Husband was in the lab when the wall was breached…"

"Aye, boy. He's the mess." The Veteran confirmed.

The Assistant bolted from the bar, chemicals swirling in his bloodstream.

"They'll be wanting to talk to you!" The Veteran called after him.

Surveying what was remaining in the bar, the Veteran helped himself to the Assistant's forgotten beer, and peered out over the crowd. A familiar back was sitting at a table talking to that mature, long-legged, red-haired, light-eyed Vixen the Veteran had been coveting all these months. He couldn't quite make out the man from this angle, but the sense of familiarity was typical. The Veteran knew everyone up here. Given the confined quarters, that recognition was inevitable, but he still couldn't place it.

The Veteran only had one more day before the next transport arrived and he could finally afford to do what he really wanted, rather than run security for these Company scientists: a nice cozy teaching gig back on the ground. Summers off. Only a single class to start, teaching rich entitled youngsters the basics of what they needed to know to survive in space, so that when their jobs inevitably brought them up here they'd have a clue what was going on.

One more shift. One more night. And then he could return home to a normal life.

He took a large gulp, and turned back to the bar.

Chapter 3: The Assistant and the Investigators

The Assistant ran through stark white corridors, not noticing the people he bumped into or those who jumped out of the way to avoid him.

He ran through the small city in space. The crown jewel of Earth's capitalism and the need to keep pushing boundaries outside the prying eyes of the public. The fact that proteins could only fold into certain unique shapes, or that chemicals would only form perfect omnidirectional crystal matrices without the pull of gravity, those were merely bonuses to the utter guaranteed privacy of being in orbit.

The station's growing population had meant that the Company administrators had to accede to more than basic human needs for survival. Shops and restaurants got permission to take up a stall or a pod, for a hefty rental fee. Most businesses dug from their marketing as well as operating budgets to make it happen: having a footprint in space meant something to the human psyche, and stock prices rose accordingly.

Advertisements and a monger or two tried to catch his attention, but he was flying past them. And in no time at all, he rounded the final corner.

The Investigators were in front of the pod's airlock door, fatigued and sweaty after going through what must've been a very thorough decontamination. The Assistant heard a double hiss of air as they took off their helmets and turned curiously in his direction, watching him skid to a halt on the other end of the short hallway.

"Is he in there?! Is he?!" After a moment's hesitation the Assistant bolted and tried to barrel past them, not thinking about the practical consequences of entering the pod if it were exposed to vacuum. His mind was only on one thing: finding his Husband.

"Hold it!" The woman yelled at him as both Investigators held him back. He kept pushing with his legs, trying to overpower them, screaming incoherences.

And in an instant his mad rush of heedlessness boiled over. Wanting to die alongside his love evaporated.

He saw the hallway around him as if for the first time. A place he had walked hundreds, thousands of times. Sterile, sterile, sterile. Not lived in.

No one could call this home.

How had he?

He sank down to the ground before them, withering. "It's true, isn't it? My Husband is gone."

The male Investigator looked down at him sympathetically. "I'm afraid so. You must be the Assistant then."

He didn't affirm or deny it. He found he didn't care who he was. Numbness spread out from his chest in great veins.

After a long moment of silence he managed to find an ember of emotion; anger at the situation, at life itself, prompted his voice back into working: "Who are you? Why were you notified before I was? What gives you the right to split the lab from the station?"

Both Investigators looked at him with pity. She crouched down next to him and responded in the most compassionate voice she had: "Station operations got an alert as soon as there was a hull breach. They contacted the Company, and the Company called us. We *are* Federal Investigators, but we're working for the Company. Normally we handle things like inter-corporate disputes, breaches of contract."

"Or negotiating non-disclosures, non-competes, even data-hostage situations," the other Investigator chimed in.

"Yes, all that," she continued. "But usually the field work is done for us and we act more as analysts and facilitators. Because our positions are with the ground-side government it lends us a weight of authority — the corporations know any deal we work out with them will be binding and legitimized if it ever gets back to a court on Earth."

A look of shocked dismay spread across the Assistant's face. "You're…you're lawyers?!"

She shrugged. "We spend most of our time in orbit nowadays. That means we were already out of the gravity well when the call came in."

"Which means you were cheaper to transport here," the Assistant sneered. "But why hire you at all? What about station security?"

The male Investigator now took the lead: "For minor infractions, sure. But this looked like a potential homicide to the damage — sorry what're they called? The *perception* control team. The Company knows that to maintain its sovereignty without oversight from the ground they need a more trustworthy source for a case like this. An impartial third party."

"But you just said…you're the farthest thing from impartial! The Company must be paying you huge bonuses on top of your government salaries!" The Assistant felt his frustration ebb as he realized the universe still worked the same way it always had: "Appearances. It's appearances. You're impartial *on paper* according to your resumes, and that's all that matters."

She sighed. "Just so. And now that we've answered your questions, can you answer some for us? Do you know what happened here?"

"The Doc, my Husband, some kind of a fight, now they're both dead," he managed to croak out.

"That's right. Well, it's what we think. You don't know if the Doc had a spacesuit with him, do you?"

The Assistant looked up at that. "No. Why would he?"

The male Investigator looked over to his partner, shrugging. She moved a hand through her hair to finally free it from the constrains of her suit and asked, "Is there anything else you can tell us that might help? Did they have a history of fighting? Were either of them violent?"

"No, no. Neither were aggressive at all. Why would they fight? We all worked together happily for years." He felt his porcelain visage begin to crack under the weight of those memories.

"And what were you working on?"

A sudden stiffness straightened his spine. His muscles hardened again as he looked up at them for the first time. "You know I can't tell you that." Unknowingly, their questions had steered his consciousness to an inkling of an idea that now tickled him: why *did* they fight? *Cui bono?*

"The Company will have to let us know everything eventually. It's vital to the investigation. You might as well save us the hassle of filling out the paperwork and having to wait for a response."

The Assistant shook his head. "No, you'll never find out. It's a waste of time to even try." Strength was slowly returning after his sustained sprint and subsequent crash. "I've lost everything today. But I'll lose even more if I tell you anything about what we were working on in there." He stood up and meekly excused himself: "I have to go."

The Investigators wanted to press him further. But they both knew he was grieving, that his mixed up emotions and clouded thoughts would clear only with the passage of time. So they'd get back to him later. They were trapped on this station together. Where could he run that they couldn't find?

They watched him walk away without another word.

Chapter 4: The Assistant

Rage welled inside him.

As his unadulterated love once had, rage erupted from him sporadically like a geyser — at moments he felt an almost serene nothingness, and then a burst of hate and anger and frustration controlled him as surely as an engineer programming a robot. He had barely stayed calm for the Investigators after his initial outburst, but back here in the slate confines of his angular room, his emotions got the best of him.

He smelled a shirt, lonely on the desolate, dark floor, and eventually its scent brought forth the imprisoned tears the Assistant thought he had locked away. And while weeping, presently, he slept.

When he awoke, his mind, previously so fragmented by his traumatic state, was whole again.

He now had a clear end-goal, he just wasn't sure where to start. He agreed with the Investigators that it had been a crime of passion. That the Doc hadn't brought a suit with him into the lab. But he had information they lacked. He knew what morbid curiosities had been brought to life in that lab, what they had ultimately been working toward. And he suspected something they would never guess: why the radar would be unable to find body-sized debris floating outside.

His revenge, that tight ball of determination twisting in his gut, pulsed in time with his thumping blood.

He had a hunch — only a hunch — on which he was about to stake *everything*.

Chapter 5: The Mouse and the Princess

The Mouse was not happy with an ordinary life, but that's exactly what it was turning out to be.

She once dreamed of being an astronaut. One of the few to brave the radiation and micro-meteorites for the pursuit of science and personal glory. But laziness and an affinity for blaming others rather than improving herself had defeated ambition on a meandering path of mediocrity, eventually leading here, to this coffee shop in Ann Arbor, Michigan. It was cozy and warm in an artificial fireplace kind of way.

The Mouse wasn't wearing headphones or intently staring at a laptop screen, nor were her eyes flicking across the pages of a novel. She was demurely sipping a part-espresso part-milk part-added-flavor drink of commercialism manifest hoping, as she always hoped, that someone, anyone would notice her and she could make a new friend. A dedicated, common soul to bond with. Someone she had more overlapping interests with than—

"Hey!" hollered the Princess, with her perfect smile and perfect strut, as she waved and strode over.

"Hi," was the Mouse's timid reply.

The Princess set her bag down and on her way to the coffee shop counter said, "I'll just be a sec, OK?"

The Mouse fumed silently while she waited. Even for an outing as casual as grabbing coffee with a friend, the Princess was dressed to the nines and fashionably late. Everything she wore was tight and bright and accentuated her positive assets. The Mouse, on the other hand, dressed simply for comfort. She idly mused about how much time she had saved across the years of her life compared to the Princess by not taking hours to get ready each morning. And if they would even be friends if it weren't for growing up together. But they *had* grown up together, so closely that they knew each other's true names, and the Mouse tolerated the Princess's idiosyncrasies.

"So I couldn't score a free drink today. That trivia question was too hard! I don't know what happens in the news here on Earth, let alone in outer space."

The Mouse rolled her eyes: "You're kidding. It's everywhere. The first murder in space!"

The Princess smacked her lips. "Oh that's right. *You* think that's where the future's headed. That we'll *all* have to go into space eventually. Because that's where we can get more precious metals for jewelry once we run out on Earth."

"Yeah…jewelry. *That's* the reason we should be exploring the cosmos."

"I'm all for bringing costs down, but you should let someone else worry about it. Space sounds boring. Do they even have clubs? Night life? Those stations sound cramped and like they're all business. You should be glad you aren't there. Besides, it was dangerous *before* a murder happened!"

"Come on, don't you find it the least bit exciting? They say it was a crime of passion!"

"What's there to be passionate about in space? It's empty. And cold."

"But it's so full of potential! There's so much we don't know. All of that opportunity for discovery and exploration."

"So what would you do if you went up there? What could *you* contribute?"

At that the Mouse was back to her original line of reasoning before the Princess walked through the door.

And the Princess felt the emanating despair as if she were the hangman holding the noose. To alleviate her own guilt, she tried fine-tuning the topic: "Have you registered for classes yet? I hear there's a new professor who retired from working in space and he'll be here in time to teach this semester. If you take his class and do well, maybe he'll give you some advice or write you a recommendation."

The words trailed away in the Mouse's mind and she was left with a softly glowing ember of hope that the Princess' suggestion could get her out of this slump. That an external force could succeed where her own internal abilities had failed.

Their drinks got cold while the Princess talked to herself about nothing and the Mouse lost herself in a future emboldened.

Chapter 6: The Veteran and the Vixen

The Veteran found himself face to face with an angel. Not an ethereal trick of the light, either. This one had lips that were a shade too red, eyelashes a fraction too long, and a friendly smile directed his way. Those things *never* happened all at once. Somewhere in the recesses of his thought patterns a tocsin was chiming out a song to counter the siren's, but it was too subtle and the sound started drowning in a sea of alcohol surrounded by a single thought: *The last shift is over. This is my last time in this stupid plastic bar. So why not?*

Not wanting to botch his chances with a cheesy opening line, the Veteran waited for her to make the first move. After a moment of intent staring he was rewarded for his restraint when she scooted beside him, giving a profile view of a dress a tad too tight. It was backless, tasteful, and timeless. It made him think about how he would be able to see all that milky skin if her lustrous hair weren't flowing over her shoulders in the warm shades of sunrise.

She set down a martini she obviously hadn't touched, and turned to him. "I hear it's your last night. The fresh troops get here tomorrow and you take their ride back?"

"Something like that."

"Funny. I was planning to return for a spell. Think there's a private room open on the transport so I can ride with you?"

He almost balked at her forwardness. "Probably. There's more coming up than going down nowadays."

She clapped her hands in finality. "It's settled then!" Her pupils focused on him, black holes surrounded by bright nebulae. "And in the mean time, do you have any plans for your goodbye hurrah? Revelry?" She had the audacity to wink at him. "Debauchery?"

At that moment, when things seemed the most surreal to the Veteran, he felt that reliable instinct — which had saved his life numerous times on the battlefield — push through his self-inflicted haze and demand some recognition. One thing fell into place, which he couldn't ignore: "That man earlier, sitting with you over there, who was he?"

"You sure have a good memory," she quipped. "He's a business associate of mine. A purely professional arrangement."

His eyes narrowed slightly at the evasion. "And what business are you in again?"

"I'm a journalist. I came up to interview some of the more prominent scientists." She flipped a switch from serious to playful. "But why get into the details of our lives right now? We have a while before the flight to get to know each other. And in more...private circumstances."

And so, his defenses defeated by her simple persistence, he thought for the second and final time: *Why not?*

Chapter 7: The Major General and the Investigators

The Major General knew something was wrong. Before the static ever resolved into faces a suspicious chill settled on his spine, and this conversation was doing nothing to dislodge it.

The Investigators were reliable folk. He tried putting himself in their shoes. Away from his polished, tastefully expensive office and stuck in the middle of the void. Not wearing a crisp uniform his Orderly was responsible for each day so he could focus on the fundamentals of pushing paper around. Not being treated like a middle manager in the United States Air Force, which still claimed it was in charge of national space defense, despite the fact that space remained demilitarized by agreement to an old United Nations treaty. Not getting stuck with liaison duty between the government and their investigation. Not being the one whose pension was on the line if this fiasco turned sour. Well, it was already pretty rancid, with the suspect's body missing. He doubted it could smell much worse.

The Investigators disagreed.

The man was talking: "Look boss, we've got really bizarre stuff going on up here. We ordered the lab pod disengaged from the station, but it appears that a *second* pod has also been detached, this one a large multi-family apartment unit. There aren't any reports of missing persons or equipment yet though."

Compared to everything else, this seemed mild. The Major General took it in stride: "So could it be an error with executing the order? Some operator pushed two buttons when it should have been one?"

The woman spoke up: "No one is claiming responsibility, sir, but it is a possibility. We're trying to keep an open mind. And there is one remote explanation that we wanted to get your opinion on." She turned her head to her slightly out of focus partner, a worried expression furrowing her brow.

"We're working with incomplete information here, boss," started the man as the Major General impatiently watched the screen. "We know when the suspect and the victim's shift started in the lab, but until the station detected the breach, anything could have happened in there." Now he was rambling. "And they had been working in there for months. There would have been lots of opportunities to prepare or stash something. Hide a weapon…or a suit."

The Major General had heard enough dancing around the point: "Out with it! I'll hear your idea before I judge it. Don't assume I'm about to lynch you for some creative thinking."

Reassured, the woman took over. "The crux is this, sir: despite our initial impressions that this was not premeditated, we believe there's a non-zero chance the Doc is alive. He could have done an exceptional job covering his tracks and faking his own death. It would explain why we never got a blip on his body, and he could be using the apartment pod as a hideout. The biggest hole in our theory — besides a lack of supporting evidence — is that as soon as each pod separated from the station, it lost power. There's no life support."

"But if he survived going into space from the lab, then he presumably still has a working suit."

"Yes, sir. But he would need to be re-supplied. Power, oxygen, food, water. And if he's been back on the station since the incident there's been no hint of it, no log anywhere in the system, no rumors."

"However unlikely this scenario is, you two have to pursue it. If this man is still alive then you *must* find him. And the sooner the better. The instant the next personnel transport arrives, if anyone else suspects this, you can be sure you won't be the only ones searching for him. And some of those others — perhaps his employer — will want to do a lot more than question him if he's alive."

"Yes, sir. We'll both keep our eyes peeled." The woman gathered herself for a moment before continuing, "And sir, there's more bothering me. Everyone here has been tight-lipped about the research — it's all the highest level of non-disclosure and confidentiality. Plus, it's not like there's a nearby court that can subpoena anyone. So…do you have any information on what they were working on? Any insights or clues we might not have? Anything at all would be useful at this point."

The Major General had known this was coming. "It's not much better here, I'm afraid. *All* of the work on that station is private Company business. A lot of pharmaceuticals. Some of our own defense contractors. Superconductor and electronics hardware R and D. But every time I inquire about this lab a report comes back saying it's above my pay-grade or beyond my clearance level. I'm looking into some back-door channels to help me out, but for the time being I'm as in the dark as you. It's not all friendly in this bureaucracy. Half of the higher-ups are trying to shut me down while the other half are yelling at me to pursue this at full speed."

"And the transport, sir? It's going to make our jobs harder with all those extra personalities up here."

"I did my best to block them, but it's still free space. There's nothing we can do legally."

The man took his turn: "And those wishing to return, boss? Can we hold them?"

The Major General shifted in his seat and shook his head. "Again, no. We don't have the jurisdiction. I'm trying to…*suggest* a course of action to the Company. It's difficult. They don't want to stall their work. Profits and all."

"Could we hold them on the surface? At least until we know the full story behind the lab? Call it a health and safety measure?"

"We do have a presence at the landing site." The edge's of the Major General's lips curled slightly upward in the promise of a toothy grin. "However, I think it would be far better to put the passengers through the usual screenings and then monitor them from a comfortable distance. There are a multitude of three-letter acronyms that would love to aid us in this department. We don't need to show our hand and expose ourselves or the extent of our resources until we determine if this is an isolated incident."

The woman smirked. "Very clever, sir. But there are a dozen stations transporting materials and personnel between themselves and Earth on a weekly basis. We're having trouble with one homicide — we aren't equipped to handle anything more. What if it turns out this isn't an isolated incident? "

The Major General realized the pit in his stomach was gone. Maybe this situation was still fresh enough to whip into an opportunity after all. "Then, in that case, I will see about expanding our jurisdiction."

Chapter 8: The Mouse and the Veteran

The Veteran's biceps were as large as the Mouse's thighs, and his hard eyes looked comfortable with command, exposing a personality used to dominating, giving orders and having them followed without question, backed up by a body to match.

In her daydream, the Mouse was sitting exactly where she currently sat — in a clammy plastic desk in this nondescript classroom. But unlike real life, she and the Veteran were alone, without all the other half-awake, half-hungover students scattered throughout the room. And she was wearing a low-cut V-neck sweater with a plaid skirt instead of an unwashed hoodie and a pair of lightly stained jeans.

The Veteran would tell her how he could help her improve her grades, her future, her life — if she were willing to pay the price. And she would hint that she'd be willing to do *anything* as she got out of the desk and with purely fictional confidence approached him as if she were the predator instead of the prey. She would let him make the first move and place his hand on her covered shoulder, gently pushing her backward until she leaned against the large desk at the front of the room. Then he would move his hand to her knee, sliding it slowly up the outside of her leg, his calloused fingertips rough against her skin. When she didn't stop him he would finally grab her with both hands and forcefully throw her onto her back on top of the desk. He'd begin hiking up her skirt while leaning over her and going in for a kiss, breath hot and humid, lips parted in anticipation—

Her illusion shattered. His face looked scratchy with its several days of unshaven prickly hairs sticking out. A couple of his teeth had a painfully sharp edge to them. And despite his obvious stature of strength, his skin had an unnatural hue — a paleness that bordered on translucent. The overall appearance of the Veteran was not unappealing, but it wasn't one she entirely trusted.

As the heat in her body dropped from scalding to room temperature the Mouse realized that this all stemmed from the rumors. The very rumors the Princess had repeated to her last night. Everyone knew the Veteran had returned from a private space station, a frontier without laws or rules. Combine that with the fact that this was his first time teaching, and it meant he hadn't yet acclimated to how political an environment the University could be. So instead of carrying out his student love affairs privately, discretely, and with only one lover at a time — like the other professors did — he had established a sort of sex club. An elite group of hand-picked horny undergrads — both guys and girls — who once initiated by the Veteran all hung around his off-campus house and screwed in wild night-long parties.

Or so it was rumored. The Princess had eked it all out somehow, and promised to put in a good word if she happened to get invited. There *were* an unusually large number of students absent; skipping class was a part of college life. But not en masse. Of course, it could be coincidence. Exaggeration. The Mouse couldn't be sure of the truth behind any of it unless she were there to witness, or in an extremely unlikely (but exciting) turn of events, participate. And while her thrill at the thought of being with the Veteran may be a fantasy, the Mouse was still certain of one thing: she wanted in, if only to confirm that she could be a part of something mysterious and exclusive.

Chapter 9: The Assistant

The fist retracted as soon as it landed the blow. The punching bag indented for a brief second, before its insides adjusted to fill the cylinder again. By that time, another fist had replaced the first.

The Assistant knew that impulse was at least as important as force when throwing a punch; that damage caused was greater when his hand didn't linger to help absorb the impact. But he also knew that with his physique his broad shoulders were his greatest asset, so he put the full weight behind them into every strike.

In these moments his stress abated and he could think with a clear mind about anything other than the present circumstances. Alas, he was self-aware enough to know that the endorphin-induced effect during these gym sessions was only temporary.

The thought that disturbed him most as he swiftly shifted stances several times was the disappearances. Never mind that he couldn't do his job with the lab in quarantine, floating away from the station, visibly tumbling off axis through the large windows lining the workout room. Or that the Company had demanded he return on the next transport to officially debrief. That he wouldn't, couldn't follow that order yet, which would spell the end of his career. That his boredom and inability to act were consuming him faster than his grief.

No, it was the disappearances that bothered him. They were a wedge in his brain, an obstacle he couldn't see past or work around. They were the most recent and unsettling piece in this ill-defined puzzle. It may be coincidence, but it seemed to the Assistant that as soon as the apartment pod had separated and begun its frictionless journey away from the station, people had gone missing. One or two at first, hardly noticed in the confusion of a transport arriving and subsequently departing. But then personnel no longer showed up for work at an accelerating pace. Yet, no bodies found, no suits unaccounted for.

And people's imaginations had been working overtime to compensate. The Investigators were clueless, offering no insight. The general consensus at the bar, where the Assistant only listened and never spoke, was of a new religious cult taking up residence in the abandoned apartment pod. That they had some independent power source — solar panels most likely — along with private suits and transportation. This station was their staging ground, and once shown the light the secrets of the universe were so powerful that anyone listening was eager to give up their day job to join. A minority view held that it was a new form of space-dementia, and the radar had been fixed not to report all the suicides it found in the deep black, in order to keep up moral.

The Assistant didn't ascribe to either conspiracy theory. He did think that the Doc was at the center of it, whatever *it* was. And that it wouldn't be slowing down any time soon.

Practically, all it meant was that the Investigators remained bewildered, the industry work was grinding to a halt until a large batch of replacements arrived on the next transport, and the Assistant was stuck with a personal vendetta he couldn't fulfill.

As he was wrapping up his footwork exercises, a glimmer outside caught the Assistant's peripheral vision. He stopped moving and approached the window to get a better look at the source: a quickly shrinking ball of flame where the lab pod had been. The silent explosion shifted from a bright white light to yellow, then orange, before finally dispersing into dust and debris. Too shocked to comprehend what had happened, his only thought was that his Husband's frozen remains were now scattered motes of organic material, dissolving into the void.

Then a long overdue thought crept into his brain during this new feeling of vulnerability: *I need more friends up here.*

And I need them now.

Chapter 10: The Major General and the Orderly

The Orderly placed the dinner tray in front of the Major General, the steak still steaming with heat and moisture.

The Major General smiled and picked up his napkin, careful to place it properly to protect his crisp and clean uniform before reaching for his fork and knife.

Just as the Orderly reached the door, the Major General said, "Stay a bit, will you? I have some things I want to run by you."

"Certainly, sir," came the stoic response as the Orderly closed the door and turned back to face the Major General.

"Well, take a seat," the Major General said right before he finished making a very satisfying cut and placing the resulting large chunk of red meat on his tongue.

"Thank you, sir." The Orderly sat down, the substantial desk between them.

For a minute, there was only unhurried chewing.

"So," began the Major General. "Our support made it on board?"

"Yes, sir. The transport will be docking at the station shortly."

The Major General gnawed away at the beef while contemplating the support he was sending. He desperately wanted to inform the Investigators that they were not alone, but knew it could prove fatal to their new undercover comrade. The Investigators were not trained in covert operations or the arts of stealth and secrecy. They were the obvious team doing the legitimate work. And if it ended up to be fruitful, all the better. He had ordered them to infiltrate the seemingly lifeless apartment pod, or at least contact whatever this underground community was. He firmly believed that whether it was religious, alien, or paramilitary, it didn't matter. But it had to be *something* because people didn't just go missing without leaving bodies behind.

Thus he was innately pessimistic about the Investigators' chances of success. Hence the unannounced and secret support that would rely on the assumption that amateurs were ultimately behind this and would therefore only be worried about the red herring Investigators. The Major General didn't like competing teams, especially when one didn't know about the other, but he felt trapped by the strangeness and lack of intelligence surrounding the whole situation. Now it was a waiting game to see if there were any demands, or if a body bumped into a bulkhead, or if the Investigators or his surprise weapon actually got to the bottom of this never-breaking case.

But in the meantime, he was going to prepare for the worst. Looking up from his food to the patient Orderly, the Major General finally voiced what he had been contemplating for years. Only now did he have the justification and the motivation. "I need you to open a new project file for me."

"Regarding what, sir?"

He would either be heralded as a hero or court marshaled depending on how this went.

"Dig up our archived plans for making a military vessel that operates in space." The Orderly's left eyebrow moved significantly at that. "And do it *quietly*. There was significant thought put into this during the Cold War, and I don't want us to repeat ourselves. Several prototypes were made and tested. Start with the X-37 project. I need the hard details. Blueprints and schematics. Calculate required natural resources, time to manufacture, and operating manpower for a squadron." The Major General paused to gulp down the last large piece of meat. "Also, find a list of names both for people to update the engineering with modern technology and for possible crew members. Don't contact another living person about this. Just use the computers. And I need it all ASAP."

"Are we fighting a war, sir?"

"Not yet."

"Then are you finished with your lunch?"

After wiping his mouth, the Major General dropped his napkin on the tray and nodded. The Orderly removed the tray and walked purposefully out the door.

The risk-averse side of the Major General hoped this new project would end up being a waste of time for both of them. His other side knew better.

Chapter 11: The Mouse, the Princess, and the Veteran

The house had a musky odor. The kind that lingers after sex, often mingled with latex and stale beer on college campuses. But that wasn't the case here: the scent was *pure.*

The Mouse was a step behind the Princess entering through the unlocked front door. They were both dressed ready for an intimate evening. The Princess tall in sable boots and a matching sleek skirt, with a frilly white top that featured a plunging neckline. The Mouse was more conservative, thin in a sunflower summer dress that was quickly losing its season.

Taking in more than the smell, the Mouse realized this house was incredible sheerly for its normalcy. Bright lighting in the foyer revealed a curving banister and staircase. Middle-class art and assemble-yourself furniture filled out the room. It was as if the home had been decorated based on magazine advertisements instead of by someone who actually had to live here.

"Hello?" the Princess called, her greeting echoing back to them.

Straining to catch a reply, they heard muffled voices coming from upstairs.

"Let's go up," the Princess said as she led the way.

Down a corridor that stretched the length of the house, the Mouse could hear various mutterings from behind closed doors. One room sounded like inconsequential small talk. Another a heated discussion. A third held grunts and moans.

At the end of the hallway a set of double doors opened into a living room where twenty or so students were lounging about, some sitting on chair arms or leaning against the walls. They were all listening intently to the Veteran, who sat in a centered throne-like leather chair, and stopped his speech as the two entered.

"It looks like we have some new faces joining us tonight." He greedily ogled the Mouse and the Princess, his gaze slowly moving up and down over every inch of each of them. Twenty other pairs of eyes followed. The Mouse was decidedly uncomfortable, but the Princess was soaking in the attention: a human solar panel at high noon.

While she was getting checked out the Mouse used the time to inspect everyone else more closely, and noticed there was an unusually high amount of hooded sweatshirts adorning the others, especially considering the balmy weather. She shook off the thought and focused on the Veteran as he started speaking again.

"Welcome." He gestured around the room. "Find yourselves a seat. I'm sure we'll all know each other by the end of the evening."

As the Mouse settled in she tried to see his face clearly, but it was strangely shadowed, as if he absorbed all the light in the room.

"This is not a religion. Not a cult. This is a club for those who seek to better themselves. For anyone who thinks that the human race should be improved, and is willing to help with that personally. This is not a place for the cool kids to get more popular, for the rich to gain more assets. This is not a frat. It's an experience. A permanent, life-changing event for those with the desire to see it through. You will not achieve nirvana, but you will be elevated.

"This is not an equalizer, not communism. What transpires behind these doors may trap you, may free you. It may make you an outcast to those who do not understand us. It may be that you are finally accepted. Whatever bonds you have now, be prepared to sever them. If you expect the worst in this time of transition there will be no surprises.

"Do not believe the suspicions of coincidence. There have been no disappearances. No one is missing. No one is lost. But there are those who cannot adjust. Whose psyches bend, sometimes break under the pressures of change. Those that can be helped are. We are not in the business of force. The first step is a choice. The last step also. We make no distinctions.

"We are responsible for creating a new class. A superior breed. All you are is your body. All you have is your soul. In changing one we alter the other.

"You are all in a dream. This is merely the path to waking yourself up."

The Mouse looked over to the Princess and saw that she was enraptured. The little respect she had left for the Princess's intellect evaporated. The Mouse needed more concrete answers before committing herself, not a practiced monologue that could've come from a B-grade sci-fi movie. She still might glean some useful tidbits, so she kept quiet and continued listening.

"Those of you whom I've spoken with privately, who are to become our members, leave with me now and you will be Initiated into our ranks amidst ecstasy," commanded the Veteran. At that, a handful of young disciples, three girls and a boy, departed ahead of him. The Mouse noticed that despite his claims of not discriminating, those four were among the most attractive of the assembled group — the boy with a rigid jawline and bright eyes, the girls nubile with curves in all the right places. Her heart sank as she realized she had only been lying to herself. To think she could belong here! The whole spiel was a charade poorly masking the reinforcement of old stereotypes.

When the Veteran reached the door he put a hand on the frame and looked back across the silent, attentive room. "Please," he smiled. "The rest of you head downstairs to the kitchen. There are some refreshments for you, and there will be some of our Initiates for you to mingle with. They can help you decide if this is the right path for you at this time." The Veteran moved into the hallway, and the room's silence burst into excited chatter.

"Come on, let's go!" the Princess urged as she tugged at the Mouse. Being closest to the door they were the first ones out and on their way back through the hallway.

"I think I might go home," the Mouse began.

But the Princess wouldn't hear it: "Don't be silly. Pass up free food?" She pointedly leered at a couple of the others with a twinkle of lust in her eyes. "And even if you don't decide to join this is shaping up to be a great mixer. You can expand your social network!"

The Mouse rolled her eyes at the Princess's ever-present opportunism.

In the kitchen they discovered hors d'oeuvres of fresh fruit and pungent cheese. Their new hosts were a half-dozen of the Initiates. The Mouse felt a strange sensation in her stomach when she looked at them, very much like she was trapped in a cage with hungry lions. When they smiled, all of them revealed mouths inset with sharp teeth, a few looking almost as if they had been filed to a point. It was a frightening thought, and gave her further pause. She began wondering if the ceremony was more than sex: *Does it involve extreme body modification? Or mandatory tattoos, hidden somewhere intimate?* The ideas only further piqued her curiosity about the whole thing. She felt herself start to be lured into the mystery of the bizarre situation she found herself in.

Taking a closer look, the Mouse also noticed that all the Initiates had skin almost pale enough to match their teeth. A couple had a rosy glow to their cheeks, as if recently flushed with exercise. The Veteran might be keeping them on a tight leash inside the house. Maybe that's where some of the rumors of missing students started. These fools were probably skipping class or work to party with the Veteran as much as possible.

The Princess was already flirting with one of the Initiates. The Mouse almost felt bad for the other girls in the room as she tore into some Havarti. Against the Princess, in this game, they didn't stand a chance.

Chapter 12: The Agent

The Agent moved with a grace that belied years of training. It began with ballet and gymnastics in those formative years when the body was still flexible beyond adults' belief. The repetitive training had solidified into muscle memory that still influenced the Agent's every motion.

Her dark, narrow eyes caught everything in sweeping arcs as she stepped leisurely down the station's main corridor. She was coming straight from the newly docked transport, and noticed the obvious and predicted sparseness in the population due to the still confounding disappearances. She knew it would be even more acutely felt when foot traffic to and from the planetary transport ceased.

On the flight over, she marked those most likely to be her equivalent from another government. Most of them would wait for verification of some sort, so her advantage would be in moving quickly. As for what to do with the bodies when it was over, her superiors had a high ranking mole inside the Company, and they told her how the first one died in great, emotionless detail. There hadn't been a corpse found since the murder that sparked this investigation, but that didn't mean there wouldn't be any more, which meant she could hide the remains of any rival in plain sight if she prepared them properly.

With her tied-back jet-black hair, taut slacks, and dress shirt, the Agent easily blended in with the various suits also heading from the airlock to the living section, but she specifically avoided wearing a jacket so as not to constrict her movement.

One of her marks, a taller dark female with braided hair, obnoxiously American, was about twenty paces behind. The Agent wasn't even going to bother getting settled in before dealing with this first task. She ducked into a public restroom, checked that it wasn't occupied, and then counted in her head for every step the woman behind her would make. At the exact moment required, the Agent opened the door and yanked the woman inside, slamming her head against the wall. She made a final, crushing blow, but was deflected enough at the last instant by her quickly recovering victim to rob her move of its fatality and thus deny her a quick victory.

Except for the sounds of heaves and grunts and contact between flesh, no noise was made by either. Whoever emerged victorious would not want anyone else to be aware of this battle.

The Agent felt her opponent get in several good strikes to her midsection, bruising, but not doing any permanent damage. She bode her time, knowing that the first surprise attack would take its toll, and so conserved energy, waiting for an opening. When it came a few moments later the woman had just missed a whirling kick and — her equilibrium probably still reeling from the recent trauma — she fell to a knee off balance. The Agent steadied the woman's head with her left hand and punched through the trachea with her right. Sputtering and trying to breathe through a shattered windpipe, the woman eventually died of asphyxiation with a look of surprise in her eyes.

The Agent matter-of-factly went about scrubbing down the scene: after putting on a pair of gloves, she cleaned the woman's nails to remove scrapes of her own skin, washed off blood on the woman's knuckles from her own split lip, and using a hand-held electronic motor with a suction tube attached, she cleaned off the woman's clothes in case of any stranded hairs or eyelashes.

Confident in her work, the Agent then took out a molded set of artificial teeth that could be worn on her hand like a glove. She violently clenched her fist around the body's neck and tore a large chunk of flesh out. That skin and muscle she tossed into a toilet and flushed. Deception complete, she then removed the gloves and flushed those as well.

The Agent returned to the hallway and looked up and down the length of it to make sure it was empty. The fight had presumably gone unnoticed. She turned to the bathroom door, and using a simple pick, locked it from the outside.

The Agent still had to worry about the security feeds from cameras in the hallways, but if things continued apace she might be finished before anyone thought to look.

Chapter 13: The Assistant becomes the Renegade

When the lab exploded something snapped in his head and he realized he had to stop worrying about his morals and start planning. He then gave himself a simple goal: get ten others to join him and commit to defending each other from this unknown threat.

It was now widely believed that most of those disappearing were not dead or departed, but changed, transformed somehow, occasionally returning to ominously ask a lover or coworker to join them. Most agreed to leave, out of nothing else than sheer curiosity, sharply accentuated by the boredom that set in as the station became more and more deserted. Space was lonely, and people were desperate. Those that denied the summons of the others had chilling ghost stories to tell.

The Assistant was convinced there was a tangible — and very human — explanation for all this, and his voice of reason compounded by his closeness to the murder and some good old-fashioned fear-mongering gave him the credence needed to start recruiting.

Most were simply persuaded verbally in hushed conversations, but a few had needed assurance of a different kind. Money didn't matter: everyone on the station had more than enough waiting for them back home. So where being positive didn't work he resorted to overt threats, and one time, violence. Despite his attempt at mental clarity, the Assistant still found himself trying to justify those cases to himself: it wasn't wrong if his very survival was at stake.

Tired of convincing himself of the validity of his own actions, he looked around the room of supporters he had gathered. They were gruff men and tough women. He needed people that could take care of themselves, handle a fight if it came to that. They weren't ideal, but at least there was some muscle spread around the group.

He cautioned them against congregating, but this announcement was far too important and urgent to wait on. And this way he could be sure they all got the message delivered without any unintended spin.

"This is still known to only a few people, but you all need to hear it now: I just received a message from the Investigators telling me that there have been three more murders." The Assistant expected a clamor or uproar, but the group remained stone-faced. He had chosen well.

"All three were replacements from the most recent shuttle. All the bodies were found with the same wound as my...as the first. In response, the Company has enacted a quarantine, effective immediately. Inter-station travel is still allowed, but we can't go home to Earth. Not until this mystery is solved. The Investigators don't know who did this, but I'm confident that *we* do. The Doc was the primary suspect in one murder, but they discount the idea of him for these most recent ones because they think that in all likelihood he died without a suit in space. Based on what I told some of you about our work in the lab, you may already have guessed how this reasoning is flawed.

"The Doc blew up our lab to keep secret a power he now hordes for himself and those he can influence. We were working on enhancements to the human genome. We weren't trying to make super soldiers or a plague, but we were working for multiple governments and high bidders.

"With Earth's dwindling natural resources and our inability to leave our solar system at any reasonable speed, the idea was to provide another option for nothing less than the continued survival of our species. Earth is the only life-supporting rock we can get to in a workable timeframe, since we would need decades or centuries and unimaginable expenses to terraform another planet or moon. How much easier to make it so that humans could survive in the vast majority of the universe as it already is: an empty vacuum with a temperature of 3 Kelvin, and no atmosphere to protect against cosmic and solar radiation.

"Although we weren't finished with the research yet, I think the Doc skipped to the end and modified himself early. He might even have been working in secret on the side or with another lab to keep some advancements only for himself. Compartmentalizing for his sole benefit. And now he's using the technology to modify others. Based on the number of disappearances he must have well over a hundred followers by now. We cannot stop them as we are. And we can't stay here." The Assistant paused to see how they would react. There were stern faces, jaws set, and a lot of nodding heads. "We'll head for another station. One with its population still intact. Begin a counter-movement there to protect ourselves. But before we go, we should salvage as much as we can from here, both in equipment and personnel. Every soul we bring with us is one more they can't add to their ranks. And that's worth something, especially up here. Now, see who you can convince and go look for anything that could be used as a weapon. Our goal is to leave tomorrow with our numbers doubled and everyone armed. See to it."

The Assistant felt a rush of power at how the others heeded his words. He was now a leader, working against his former boss and country, even the Company. A true Renegade.

He moved around the dispersing group, giving individual assurances and instructions where needed. He didn't have a plan, but he knew it needed to look like he did.

Chapter 14: The Mouse and the Princess

The Mouse was scurrying across the quad, hands full of books and papers, when she bumped into the Princess.

"Hey, haven't seen you in a while." The Mouse looked over her friend and saw a haggard shell of her former self. The Princess was sans makeup, in clothes a few days old. Even her precious hair was in disarray. A leaf had affixed itself to the top of her head, creating a crooked crown. "You...you look awful."

The Princess forced a smile. "And here I thought you weren't one for appearances." She put up a hand to preemptively stop the Mouse from arguing. "It doesn't matter. I *feel* great. You should come back to the Veteran's house with me. You don't realize what you're missing. Being with the Initiates, hearing how they perceive the world — it's like falling in love with a bunch of people all at once." She motioned to indicate her own unkempt state. "This feels unimportant by comparison."

"Love, huh? I bet *all* the guys in there tell you it's love."

"It's about more than sex. And besides, I haven't slept with any of the Initiates yet. I'm not infatuated with them. I just want to join them, be a part of what they have."

"And they're pulling you out of class all hours of the day to do this. Aren't they?"

The Princess's smile slipped away. "No, I don't go to class much, but it's because during the day is the only time I can sleep. The Veteran's house only comes alive after dark."

There was an awkward pause as both girls had the simultaneous epiphany that they weren't a critical part of each others' lives any more. This was a much more devastating thought for the Mouse, as she now felt totally alone in the world, abandoned by even the one she trusted most. And it had happened so quickly, she hadn't understood what was changing fast enough to prevent it.

The Princess was the one to break the silence with an attempt at bridge building: "I'm starving. You want to join me for some grub?" As she spoke the Princess unconsciously pulled her hair back out of habit, and the Mouse noticed a score of scabs — some fresh, some not — decorating the Princess's neck, mostly concealed by a conspicuous turtleneck.

"What are those?" She stepped in for a closer inspection as the Princess shied away, embarrassed. "Has the Veteran been torturing you before he lets you in? Is this part of the initiation ceremony?" The Mouse's raised voice generated stares from the other students passing by, but she ignored them, too concerned for her friend's welfare to care.

The Princess grabbed her by the shoulders and sat her down on a low concrete wall nearby, and then said in hushed tones, "No! It's not abuse. I wanted this. And there is no ceremony, only understanding. I needed this to know what I was getting into." The Princess looked right into the Mouse's eyes. "Please don't judge me. I've never wanted anything more in my entire life."

The Mouse scoffed and harsh words rained down out of her like hail, unable to be forced back up into the sky: "Fine. But I won't be a part of what you're doing to yourself. Do you realize you're starting to sound like him? Now leave me alone." She shrugged out of the Princess's touch.

The Princess slowly stood and starting walking away, glancing back once with an apologetic look on her face. The Mouse remained utterly still until she was out of sight, then promptly fled in the opposite direction, back to the safety and comfort of her lonely bedroom, to weep for her lost friend.

Chapter 15: The Investigators and the Renegade

The Investigators were still at a loss. The first murder had them baffled, and these other three weren't helping. Maybe if they had been trained as homicide detectives, or had a forensics team, then they might have had more luck. They both felt there was something sloppy about the first scene they found — a less professional feel to everything. But it was only evident *relative* to the more recent cases, and they could write that off as either the killer gaining proficiency or the havoc caused by explosive decompression, or both.

They had previously championed the idea of a quarantine, but now that it was finally in effect due to the additional murders it only served to compound their isolation. They were possibly the last people left in the aluminum can they reluctantly called a home. Both mulled on that fact obsessively. It emphasized how stuck they were.

The station had fewer and fewer people milling about each day, some transferring to other stations to continue working, others disappearing without a trace. All the souls on board were finding direction one way or another, which made the Investigators feel even more alone in their motionless state.

He was huffing and puffing as they jogged down the ever-more narrow corridor toward the airlock. "Is this, huh, really all, huh, that important?" He managed to wheeze between breaths.

"Yes, you idiot. If we don't catch the Assistant now there's a chance we'll never talk to him again. He's the linchpin to this whole situation. I'm sure of it." She was breathing easy, having kept herself in shape these past few weeks. It required a lot more time and devotion in space, but those were things she had aplenty right now.

They rounded a corner and saw a large commotion around the portal to the last remaining shuttle. There were about two dozen civilians milling about: some lifting boxes, some ushering people this way or that, and some armed.

The Investigators found who they were looking for straight away. The Assistant was at the center of everything. They had heard his widely publicized plan, everyone had, which was entirely his intention. He was leaving, and taking whoever and whatever he could with him. The Investigators knew it was because the people didn't feel safe here any longer. But they both felt there must be something deeper, a gem of insight so keen it would reveal a way to unravel the whole case. All they had to do was get him talking.

"Excuse me," she began, touching the Assistant lightly on the shoulder, turning him gently but purposefully toward her, "but where did those people get weapons? Are they registered to have them?" She wore a smug look, thinking she could get him to incriminate himself badly enough that they had cause to hold him.

"We found the weapons. The station may not have had real police, but there were a few Company security guards, and one or two of them had armories. Plus, we considered any of the traitors' personal belongings to be fair game, and a few of them were the paranoid type." The Assistant pivoted, returning to his work.

The male Investigator just looked at her and shrugged.

She knew he had admitted to something illegal. Breaking and entering at the very least, certainly. But now that she looked around she realized she couldn't hold this man — or any of them — even *with* cause. There was too much firepower held in the wrong hands. But she'd keep this going as long as she could if there was even the slightest chance she'd get some answers.

"Did you say traitors? We know about disappearances," and she indicated her partner, who was examining the dirt under his nails at that moment, "but who is betraying anything?"

The Assistant turned back, obviously annoyed: "Those disappearances — haven't you put it together yet? They're recruits. The foundation of a new army. It doesn't matter which country they came from originally, they're all traitors now."

"Whose new army would that be?"

"The Doc's. He's the one behind this."

She laughed a brief, derisive laugh. "And these gullible fools you've assembled, do they believe that as well?"

"They trust me. That's enough for most of them."

"Fine, I'll humor you. What would the Doc do with an army? And an army that's trapped in space! If there really are a hundred people living on the abandoned apartment pod then their quality of life must be abysmal. They can't have much power. They're quickly running out of oxygen and food. Worse, they don't have any transportation! You're taking the last shuttle! So if they aren't all dead now, they will be very soon."

"Your boxed in boundaries have prevented you from seeing this clearly from the start. Try thinking without constraints, without preconceptions. Why do you assume things like a lack of oxygen or food scare them? How can you be so sure they don't have a way of getting around in space without a shuttle?

"And as for what the Doc could do with an army that you say is 'trapped' in space: it's true freedom up here. There aren't police. No military presence. We're at the top of the gravity well! While the people of Earth are stuck on its surface. With a few simple thrusters or mining equipment the Doc could send a massive asteroid to any point on Earth. A big enough rock would have the same effect as a slew of nuclear bombs. He could decimate major population centers. Devastate whole industries. Wreck the global economy. And all the Doc has to do is some algebra and trigonometry."

She thought about that for a moment and came up short. They hadn't considered it viable. But if it were possible, then the threat the group of disappearing people posed was much greater than anyone but this man before them had realized. No matter their political or religious affiliation, they were dangerous. Potential terrorists. The kind of enemy the government would spare no expense to stop.

It was no longer enough that they wait out the killer's food and oxygen and power supplies. They needed to act. Now.

"Thank you for your time," She and her partner moved to leave, heads together for a confidential conversation.

"By the way, I am no longer his Assistant," he solemnly intoned, and motioned across the dwindling crowd pushing into the shuttle. "I don't follow the Doc or anyone anymore. I'm their leader now."

She saw the truth of his words in the way the others looked at him, how they stood straighter as he approached. And as the Investigators walked away, she wondered if there weren't two groups of traitors to worry about.

Chapter 16: The Agent, the Minion, and the Doc

The Agent had arrived with a discreet personal suit buried amongst her belongings. Extremely expensive, but invaluable in completing missions such as this. She had used it to cross the void between the station and the apartment pod after dispatching the last of her competition. Floating with nothing but the stars for company required fortitude, leading to panic and hysteria in those not trained for it. Her mind never wavered.

Once aboard she noticed the reports were at least true for this section: there was no power, no atmosphere. She kept the suit on. There was something eerie about this place tugging at the edges of her senses; dust disturbed where there was no air to move it.

After slinking through the bedroom and kitchen of a private apartment, she came to a large, open lounge area. All the portholes that faced the sun had conspicuously been covered, leaving only the shine of the stars to see by. And at least forty or fifty people were milling about...not a single suit to be seen on any of them.

Observing living skin exposed to vacuum was so foreign to her that she was distracted long enough for a clawed hand to nearly rip her wide open. A glimmer of starlight momentarily obscured at the corner of her vision was the only warning. She panicked, knowing the thin body-veil she wore wasn't rated for combat, but managed to dodge the fierce swipe by arching backward into a hand-spring. After righting herself she saw her attacker — a small, spry man whose features were obscured by the shadows of this ill-lit place. Without hesitating, she made a spinning kick with an outstretched leg to whip herself forward, but at the last moment pulled her leg in like a figure skater and used the angular momentum produced to power a punch at the man's face.

Her hand hit brick. His jaw should been dislocated or broken, but instead he just massaged it lightly, a minor discomfort. He started moving forward as she retreated carefully. When her last step brought her back against the wall, the man suddenly stopped and looked toward the others in the room.

A hand from the middle of the crowd was waving her forward. Her attacker saw it and fell back a few paces, allowing her to pass.

Slowly, showing more confidence than she felt, while suppressing all of the emotion welling up inside her, the Agent moved toward the beckoning hand. Once there, she saw that it belonged to a graying man in a simple jumpsuit. He looked at her for a moment, nodded, and then turned away from her and began walking out of the lounge. She followed.

After weaving through a few different hallways and hatches, they arrived at an airlock. The man ahead of her ushered her in, then closed the door behind them. The airlock cycled.

On the other side the Agent found additional rumors that were true as well. Here was a well-lit section that obviously had power, and the readout on her heads-up display reported that the atmosphere was that precious and breathable mix of nitrogen and oxygen. She took off her head-piece, which in this suit was more like throwing back a hood than taking off a helmet.

"Welcome," the man started. "You know who I am, but I'll go through the formality of introductions for the sake of ritual. Something I'm guessing you are keen on. I *am* the Doc. You just had a close encounter with my Minion. This is my haven, small though it be, we have anonymity and independence here. All of your questions will be answered in time. But first: who might you be?"

"I am the Agent. But there are other roles I have been instructed to take here."

"Such as? The Assassin perhaps?"

"On the station I assumed that title a few times."

"We knew there was someone else. My people here have only ventured out on very brief, specific missions, and we impressed on them the supreme importance of not leaving a body trail behind." He rubbed his chin thoughtfully. "You have hindered us and helped us, and it was all unintentional."

"My intention was to ensure that I was the only Ambassador to land at your feet intact."

"Ambassador?" The Doc chuckled. "My dear, we are organized here, surely. We even have some spies on board the station. And we may have prisoners of a sort. Even an hierarchy. But it is solely for purposes of survival. Not government. I have no inclinations toward building a nation up here."

"Consider me an Ambassador to only you and your people then. It is not your nation or lack thereof that I am interested in. It is my own."

"Of course, of course. And whom do you represent?"

"The Emperor of Japan in waiting."

At this the Doc's almost comical handling of this strange woman turned serious and worried. "I may not be an expert, Agent, but I do know some of my history. Japan is a democracy. Has been for a while. And when all those European countries finally traded their own constitutional monarchies for *actual* democracies, the Japanese followed suit and even got rid of their own figurehead. I'd say they're better off for it."

She had expected this. This was her moment. To shine strong, fueled by logic and persuasion, or burn out quickly in the attempt. "You are technically correct. There is no monarch *officially* recognized. But he does exist. After World War II, General MacArthur saw to it that the bloodline was left intact, despite deposing the Emperor of any real power and making Japan a weak and simpering nation of consumerists. And again, like you recalled, in another misguided attempt at 'modernization,' the referendum to finish what the Americans started was passed by those same weak-minded masses. That was the final death knell. It removed even his ceremonial duties — along with his official status."

"The Emperor and his family were twice allowed to live. Demoted to regular citizens. Encouraged to lead *normal* lives," she spat with contempt. "Since then the line has remained pure. A small detail in the news to a foreigner. Massive in its significance to me — and others like me. Our numbers grow quietly, much like your own. Many wish to see a return to better, stronger days. I am the Ambassador of that force. Sent here in person at magnificent expense to deliver a message. The Emperor wishes to embrace you and all your people. To be your first Ally when you have no friends."

"To speak for a force — even one that's not universal — is a great responsibility," he quipped. Then sighed. His smirk worn down to a tired, contemplative expression. "It would be tempting to gain even a modicum of support on the ground right now. We may *need* it before too long. But such decisions are not quickly made. I will give you an answer in time. You shall be our guest until then, and after, if you so choose, regardless of the outcome. We have many positions available for those with your training, and a great desire to fill them. You may find our offer too enticing to refuse.

"But before you think this a good sign, know that I am reluctant to side with an entity that is itself desperate for allies. I will not be the instigator of a coup. Our strength right now is in our secrecy, you must understand that."

She nodded solemnly. "We have experience in this as well. If the Emperor's plans became known to the government, or my presence here were revealed, we could lose everything. You are not the only one who risks much in this venture. Still the Chrysanthemum Throne sits empty. An Empire forgotten, leaderless. I am too much a patriot to abide that for long."

A slight smile slowly returned to the Doc's face, drawing his lips back enough to reveal two razor-pointed incisors. "Yes," he said, "I'm beginning to realize that." He looked down, considering options for a moment, then stared at her intently and continued, "I must warn you that from orbit even an empire looks small. You yourself may come to understand that and its implications in time."

The Agent was about to respond but was interrupted by the familiar hiss of the airlock. The same Minion who had attacked her earlier revealed himself from behind the door and walked directly to them.

"Hey Doc," he said, "We just heard that the last shuttle is away. All those overly aggressive types have finally left the station."

"Good. Do a sweep. Salvage anything useful. Find out who hasn't departed and where they stand with us. And I'll be coming along: there are a couple people I know will still be there and I'd like to chat with them myself."

The Minion moved to follow orders, glaring at the Agent on his way out.

The Agent was somewhat puzzled. "Why not move back in now that you're essentially alone?"

The Doc gave her a look that said he was more keenly aware and wise than she first suspected. "First, this is our home now. A new beginning. And second, there *will* be people returning to that station. Whether it's those that just left or someone else I don't know. But whoever comes looking, it'd be better if they didn't know where to find us, and if we had some warning of their arrival."

"I can see you've thought this through. You must be a shrewd planner indeed."

"I'm not trying to be clever, my dear Ambassador-of-the-force." He looked at her with dry-ice eyes. "I'm trying to survive."

Chapter 17: The Investigators and the Doc

The Investigators stared at each other across a table in the silent, deserted bar. They were trapped between an inability to move forward and an unwillingness to go back.

"What do we do now?" He said as he slumped in his seat, hands around an awful, self-concocted imitation of a martini.

She was filing her nails. Trying to distract herself from the empty nothingness this station had become.

"We were never meant for this. Neither of us has experience in forensics. We don't even have the equipment here to run the necessary tests. We got tapped because we were convenient. Already in the neighborhood. The *threat* of law. That's usually enough. But our bluff got called. Someone back on Earth has to appreciate that."

"The Major General?"

"No, he'll be covering his own back. We don't want to hamper his or the Air Force's ability to operate up here."

"Maybe we could work out a deal with him. The equivalent of honorable discharge with full benefits."

"The brass want answers. We didn't provide them. I don't think they'll be in a mood to hand out retirement packages. And the Major General doesn't have enough sway to swing that. He'd have offered earlier if he did."

"Space sucks. I wish we'd never come up here."

"I guess we'll have to ask for transport to be sent from whatever station is closest and work our way back down. It's time to stop putting this off and deal with it. Ripping the band-aid off fast stings at first, but at least you get it over with and move on."

"Let's get to it then."

Right as the duo started to rise from the table, a grinding metal noise vibrated throughout the station, achingly loud against the faint buzz of the electric lights.

"Okay," he began, freezing in place, "What was that?"

"Somebody docking?" She offered. He rose an eyebrow. "Poorly?"

"The Renegade probably turned around. But let's go check it out."

They jogged down the main corridor until they arrived at the airlock, just as a dozen figures were stepping out. They weren't armed, and they were all very pale. Despite the similarities, the female Investigator instantly recognized one from her case files. He was walking toward them with a quick, confident stride, both of them easily towering over his small stature.

"You're the Doc," she managed to stammer out, resounding shock quivering her voice.

"And you two are the Investigators."

They could only nod.

"I will admit that I am the perpetrator behind that first unfortunate accident you've been calling a murder. But the rest are not my work, nor the work of my people. So the question now remains: are you going to try to arrest me? Interrogate me? Do you believe that your titles or importance are still recognized on this station?"

The Investigators looked at each other. They already knew they didn't have the power to deal with more than one or two belligerents.

"No, of course not," she said. "We're obviously out-manned." She looked more closely at the individuals making up the crowd that now surrounded them. They all had some matching characteristics: pale skin, those frightening sharp teeth, and a low percentage of body fat. She didn't spot a single weapon on any of them. "But strangely, not out-gunned by the look of it."

The Doc smiled. It was meant to be heartfelt and welcoming, but came off as a menacing, predatory grin. "We are not in the business of violence. Yet with that said, I doubt you would survive an engagement with us. And although I typically have given people a choice in this matter, I can't have you two running around this station unfettered. So it comes down to this: will you join us willingly? I warn you that you will be coming with us no matter your response. I'm simply giving you the ability to dictate the manner and state in which you arrive."

The wheels were spinning in both their heads. This was an opportunity for a lot more knowledge. And being free would allow them more flexibility than being prisoners, or worse. After being resigned to losing their jobs and identities, this was a welcome option. The question the Doc was really asking was if they were idealists locked into their old ways, carrying their jobs with them everywhere, regardless of circumstance.

For him, survival was paramount. Ideals be damned.

For her, she would remain who she was through it all. True to her core. But sometimes continuing to do her job meant taking the unexpected road. It had led her to this very moment. And if it meant she had to be insincere now to keep going, so be it.

The results were the same. After a long second of peering into each other's eyes, she spoke for them both: "I think our curiosity has won out over our duties, Doc. Especially given the situation. We'll join you."

The Doc laughed, a genuine, hearty laugh. "I'm glad to hear it. And if you had spoken otherwise, I might not have believed you. After all, your curiosity is what made you Investigators in the first place. Now you only have to accept that you report to yourselves instead of some Earthly bureaucrat. For some, being fully in charge of their own destiny can be a frightening experience. Paralysis of choice *in extremis.* You may keep your titles if you wish, but be prepared for the rest of you to change forever."

And although it sounded odd, the Investigators shrugged, glad to be out of danger — physical or otherwise — for the time being.

"Thanks Doc," the man said. "Lead the way."

The Doc ushered them back through the airlock and motioned for the crowd to disperse. His people would do their sweep and he would send the shuttle back for them after he had gotten these two settled.

Initiated.

Chapter 18: The Mouse and the Princess

The Mouse was up late studying in her room alone. Always alone. It was hard to concentrate nowadays. Her emotions got the best of her, and her thoughts often wandered. She day-dreamed of ways she could have avoided this. Of paths better taken. Moments with the Princess when she felt they had a real connection. Jealousy at all the gawks and stares and cat-calls the Princess got. What others might call harassment but she desperately wanted to experience for herself. The way the Princess flaunted herself and received all the attention and made it appear so effortless. Even when remembering the worst, most despicable times, the Mouse missed the old Princess. This line of thought repeated itself just as she seemed to grasp the material she was working on, which made the process of studying a cyclical eternity.

She hadn't seen her friend since that last encounter in the quad, which haunted her still. The weather had grown colder as fall enfolded the campus. And what was normally such a pleasant time of year, colors everywhere shifting from the bright greens and blues of summer to the sunset oranges and golds of autumn, became instead a bleak reminder of what she had lost.

With failing grades and a distracted mind, the Mouse was ready to give up for the semester. Maybe the year. She wanted to return home, to the comfort of a familiar bed, and the pampering only parents can provide. A single peanut of pride was all that made her last this long.

It was quickly deteriorating.

Right as the Mouse was staring out the window into the black night while weighing her options for leaving school — going full time as a barista seemed pretty appealing just now — a knock interrupted the tapping of her pen against her paper.

She jumped a little. Her dorm room was in disarray. The Mouse had tried earlier to find a connection with some of the equally lonely college guys, at least the ones that had shown a hint of interest, but they had all ended the same way: she felt used and disappointed. Her last visitor had been one such attempt, and she hadn't bothered to clean up herself or the room since.

Hastily making herself a bit more presentable by using the pen in her hand to keep her unwashed hair in place as another knock sounded, the Mouse rushed to the door. "Coming!" she called.

And when she flung the door open, not knowing what to expect, her heart dropped from the top of its roller coaster climb, plummeting to a new low.

It was the Princess. But she looked like a drug addict going through withdrawal after a very long string of highs. The Mouse had never seen her so disheveled.

The Princess stumbled through the open door, eyes downcast, and settled on the Mouse's bed.

"Oh my god," the Mouse exclaimed. "Are you alright? What happened?"

"I'll... be fine," the Princess croaked out, her voice raspy, dehydrated.

"Here, let me get you some water." The Mouse went to her sink and filled a glass. When she returned with it, the Princess was staring at her with a peculiar gaze, not quite making eye contact, her focus a tad lower. *Is something crawling on my skin?* The Mouse felt a shiver run down her spine.

"Thanks." The Princess held the glass, but took no interest in it.

"You look exhausted. Is there anything else I can get you? What did they do to you?"

The Mouse looked at her friend with a worried expression as she sat down next to her on the bed. Her previous anger petty and already dissipating, forgotten as a morning mist in the face of her distraught friend.

The Princess finally looked up with unfocused eyes.

"There is something I want." The Princess put her hand on the Mouse's elbow and slowly but steadily moved it up until her hand started caressing the Mouse's hair. Their eyes locked, and the Mouse felt herself paralyzed by shock. This was unprecedented. Unexpected. She didn't know how to respond.

The Princess's hand turned her head and steadied it so they were facing each other on the bed. She moved her head in closer, but instead of going in for a kiss on the mouth, her dry lips and tongue began exploring the Mouse's neck.

It felt good, great, but the Mouse's gut had a twisted, wrong feeling. She gently began pushing against the Princess as she moaned, "Mmmm…that's nice…but we should…talk…about this."

In response, the Princess's hand grabbed the Mouse's shoulder with a strong grip and the Mouse felt a sting of pain in the middle of her neck.

"Stop! You're hurting me!" But her friend was oblivious to her words.

With a burst of strength thanks to adrenaline, the Mouse shoved the Princess back. Hard. She was freed, and with horror saw her own dark red blood dripping from the Princess's mouth.

The Mouse screamed, and bolted for the door.

The Princess caught her right as she got to it, and with an unnaturally strong arm, kept the Mouse from opening it. The Mouse turned to confront her friend and saw a wild, animal look in her eyes. She couldn't comprehend what was going on.

"No, no, no," the Mouse tried pleading. The Princess lunged in to continue sucking from the Mouse's neck wound. Her hands kept the Mouse's arms pinned to her sides, and the force of the Princess's body held her trapped against the door.

The Mouse began losing consciousness. Her fingertips and toes went numb. Then there was a knock on the door behind her, and a voice called out, "Hey, you okay in there?"

With a last effort of will, the Mouse yelled, "Help! Help me!"

The door flew open, throwing her and the Princess to the ground. A group of three of her dorm neighbors stood there. Laying on her stomach and staining the carpet crimson, the Mouse managed to whimper, "Help... please."

She saw the Princess scramble to stand and assess the situation with quick, efficient scouting of the group in the doorway, methodically gauging statures, presuming abilities, and extrapolating possibilities. Deciding better of a confrontation, the Princess turned, and with a sprinting start promptly threw herself out the window, shattering it with a crash.

The one who had burst through the door turned the Mouse onto her back and staggered at the sight of so much blood. Her body gave in to blackness.

Chapter 19: The Doc

The Doc called a town hall meeting. Any and all that were free from anything but the utmost important duties were *highly encouraged* to attend. He didn't know how much time he had left. If his plans worked: many, many years. Perhaps an infinite number if he continued his research. He wasn't sure of the long term affects of these changes, but perhaps they had stopped all disease, even aging itself. That had been part of his plan from the beginning, he'd just been forced to accelerate his time frame. How he wished he could have had more time before moving into this phase. But there was nothing to be done for it now, and many enemies were arrayed against him. He was certain there were those he didn't even know about, or those he confided in but shouldn't. Not that he fully trusted anyone other than himself. So he needed everyone to know. Just in case. A contingency plan. Not for him, but humanity.

He appeared to the crowd like an old man, seasoned in the way of the world, but when he spoke his voice was hale, still full of energy and dreams, not reminiscing of halcyon days gone by but instead defying impending death by speaking of the unmet future.

"I know people that don't believe in free will. Who think that all our actions are predetermined by our physiology. That because we have the genes and experiences we do, nature and nurture combine to create a deterministic being whose every choice could be perfectly predicted if only our DNA and history could be cataloged and analyzed properly.

"I can't believe that. Can't even entertain the notion. Not anymore.

"Once you have the kind of experience where you make a choice not because you want to, not because your instinct tells you to, but because your conscious mind decides to *despite* everything you feel, then the idea that you're not choosing freely, that you really could only go one way, becomes ridiculous. Maybe some people have never been on that knife-edge of a decision point before. Where you know your entire future history will be punctuated by a single moment.

"Well *I* have been there. Felt my hormones, the chemistry of my body screaming out to make a decision one way and through only the force of my will go against it.

"The *force* of will. It's called that for a reason. There's some resistance as you start but as you push through eventually you cross a threshold where you've moved beyond what the very physics of your being is telling you to do and instead your consciousness becomes action. This is the power of the word, of thought. To think that it is not the most miraculous thing about existence seems to me the worst lack of imagination possible. Think about it: through our collective human will we can reshape the universe. Take ore and filter metal from it. Combine acids and bases in beakers and we can balance pH, balance equations, balance scales, wealth, justice, balance anything. Our will can create corrosives and explosives and transport them and detonate them. Turn earth and water and air into a bomb and our faith can move — no — can *disintegrate* a mountain. Because we can move our muscles we can move the world. And now that we tear apart or fuse atoms together we can create all the different elements we want. Manipulate their structures to create new materials the universe has never seen. Because we have achieved fusion we could conceivably create a star. It's simply a matter of scale. Once the star is there planets and moons could follow. We could put the time and the effort in to move enough raw materials to the same empty void in space to literally birth a new solar system. We could do it again and again and again across generations to create a new galaxy. And the only thing stopping us is that *we don't want to.*

"The only limits I see in our capabilities is that we can't create matter or energy where there wasn't any before. We are still bound by the physical rules binding this universe together. But everything else is available to us! And that everything else is massive: it includes our entire prior history and all our possible futures. If we wanted to badly enough we could achieve anything. Anything! Make the unimaginable commonplace. Give ourselves superpowers. Eliminate disease and hunger and poverty. Build gut-wrenching, tear-bursting works of art and architecture and tell colossal stories to make all of us better, more alive. To learn more about ourselves and our place in the universe.

"But instead, because a few with more means and resources at their disposal than the rest of us want to stay on top of everyone else, want to stay in control, we are limited. Those people are not exercising their free will. They are following their evolutionary mandate to collect and horde resources, to keep them from others. To limit the range of opportunities for everyone else to avoid competition. Having the ability to act against the forces that turned us into what we are and yet not exercising it — lazily falling back to our baser natures and prescribed biology — is the gravest crime of all.

"And most people look at our tiny existence and how large it could be and then see all those with power and money and status and say to themselves, 'Yes, the possibilities are endless. But I am helpless to affect anything.' They feel trapped, like they have no choice. Staying down, quiet and out of sight, that's the easier path for their survival. But they are *choosing* to stay down, whether they realize it or not, following the same path that evolution set them on for countless eons. And it works. Those who don't stand up and rock the boat survive to reproduce and their children remain the same and so on. How limited. How *boring.*

"Despite the potential energy behind the will of billions we watch climates crumble, warmongers win, and may never realize our home among the stars. All because we're afraid of death. Because against that dark oblivion we feel there is no choice, no alternative, no reward great enough to face that peril.

"A hero is someone who is not given a choice, but makes one anyway. Who puts their very survival and genetic future at risk to convert the potential energy of their will into something devastatingly kinetic.

"That is what we're doing here today. We're choosing to not be dominated any longer. To change things, irrecoverably. And I know we can succeed.

"If we want to."

Chapter 20: The Agent becomes the Harbinger

Listening to the Doc, she felt in her flesh what he meant. Not following the standard path set out for her, not doing what was expected, what was safe. Bucking social pressures and ignoring the pleas of family to *just settle down and have babies.* She could feel her mind expanding at the possibilities. All futures branching out before her in a way they never had before. Her will not bowing to any distribution of how she should act. She realized she knew some people, a rare few, who were capable of making these true choices, of turning desire directly into action. And knowing she could now. That she wasn't trapped. That she never had been. That there was always a way out.

But she also realized that to have this epiphany, she had to be alive. That survival did matter. Because if you didn't survive you couldn't have a will to act on. The power — real palpable power — was the gamble of putting that at risk. Of knowingly putting your life on the line for an idea, an ideal.

She was lucky to be where she was when she was. To have this realization and know that she could sacrifice herself to achieve great things.

In that moment a purpose lodged itself inside her. To preserve the free will of countless others, to give them a chance to come to this same conclusion, was the noblest of callings.

She knew what she had to do. What she *wanted* to do.

That was true power.

Chapter 21: The Investigators, the Doc, and the Minion

"This is amazing." The male Investigator leaned against the wall in their private, pressurized compartment of the apartment pod.

"It's abhorrent, you mean," the woman responded from her seat on the couch, staring at a sketch she had made on the coffee table. "You realize some of those people are slaves. They may keep them well-nourished and comfortable. But they can't leave, and they're tortured daily."

"They all came here willingly though, and I don't know if I'd call a bite on the neck torture, exactly. At least some of them seem to like it," he countered.

"They had no idea what they were getting into. These creatures the Doc has transformed himself and the others into, the Initiates, they're not like us anymore. Not natural."

"Synthetic people without needing cyborg implants," he mused.

"But he couldn't convert everyone who wanted to be here, because then none of them would survive. You heard what he said, they need to consume the fluids of real, unmodified people. The changes come at a cost. There are deficiencies. And people like us are the only remedy."

"But as a consequence, they can survive in space without a suit! Their cell walls are strong enough not to boil in a vacuum. No need for oxygen tanks in space. This adaptation is a masterpiece of genetic engineering! Think of the possibilities! And the Doc is well aware of the issues. I'm sure he's working on a way to fix it so they no longer have this reliance on the blood of unchanged people. It's a great start, but his work was interrupted by his own premature transformation. He just needs more time to develop all of the associated technology."

"Those people are still slaves, even if temporarily. And we'll probably join them."

"Not if we go through the Initiation."

"I can't believe you're even considering that. We can't allow this experiment to continue any longer. We're going to put a stop to it immediately."

"How? You think there's a cure?"

She shook her head. "Even if a cure were possible, one does not exist right now, and it's the very last thing on the Doc's list of priorities."

"Then how do you propose to stop them? Kill everyone?" he said flippantly.

The stony stare she fixed him with in response halted him in his tracks.

"You...you must be joking. Even if we wanted to, the ones like the Doc, they're super strong. He was making bodies that could survive in space. Suppose a high-caliber gun could penetrate their cell walls, do you have one? With enough shots to kill every last one of them? There's over a hundred! What you're talking about is a suicide mission. Unless..." He paused for a moment and started pacing. "The lab equipment. The Doc must be medically modifying these people somehow. We just haven't seen where yet." He looked down at the sketch she had been inspecting. "That's a map of this pod! You're trying to figure out which door the transformation chamber is behind!"

She glared at him, annoyed. "Have you been paying attention at all? The Doc blew up the lab with the equipment in it. There is no hidden room. No magical chamber where these people are transformed. He specifically destroyed the evidence of what he had done. They're being changed some other way, using a different method than the Doc used on himself, I just can't figure out what it is."

"So...what *are* you trying to find on that map?" He had a very quizzical look on his face.

"You did get one thing right: the Doc's transformation was premature. Whether by accident or on purpose, we'll probably never know. But there are things he's not telling us. Secrets they're *all* keeping despite the apparent hospitality. Aside from surviving in space, we know additional ways they've changed: a need to drain biochemical resources from unchanged people in exchange for a fast metabolism that results in heightened senses, massive strength, and superior speed. But if the transformation happened before the research was complete, there could be other incidental, *accidental* changes. Have you noticed how pale they all are? That's probably a vitamin D deficiency or a problem with melanin production. What if those deficiencies are more than an inconvenience? What if they expose a fatal flaw in the new genetics of the Initiated? Have you ever seen one of them in direct sunlight? Or noticed how all of the food-slaves are kept in a very well-lit room for most of their waking hours? There are weaknesses he is keeping from us."

"The Doc did say that the original plan was to make people photosynthesize, so they could stay out in space perpetually, without the need for another energy source."

"That's my point! We know that didn't work. What if something went wrong with that part of the metamorphosis? To photosynthesize they would first have to be sensitive to sunlight, to absorb as much as possible — what if a kink that wasn't worked out is that they became *too* sensitive? Imagine how painful it would be if your skin had no protection against the sun. You'd be burned instantly, any prolonged exposure rapidly leading to heat stroke and death."

"So that map — you're trying to figure out which sides of the station are exposed to the sun? If your hunch is right, the Initiates won't ever be near direct sunlight. They'll have taken precautions. We already saw barricaded windows."

"If they don't go into the sun, I'll bring the sun to them."

"How? Blow a hole in the wall?"

He didn't expect her to respond, but she nodded.

"There's mining equipment up here. Including explosives. It's part of what makes having a bunch of anarchists around so dangerous. And why we need to stop them before anyone else dies or gets enslaved. They're forming a new society up here. At the top of Earth's gravity well. You heard the Renegade: they have the equipment to move asteroids around. Do you see the problem?"

He was pacing while she sat still, but he slowed as her logic began to sink in. He repeated the dire warning: "A few people up here with the technical know-how and a little push on a big rock in the right direction could kill millions."

"And almost everyone here is a scientist or engineer. If anyone can figure it out, they can."

"This...this is terrible." He sunk against the wall and put his head in his hands. "The Doc made it sound like paradise. He said he doesn't have political inclinations."

"And is it worth the risk to trust him? Even if he *is* telling the truth, another one of these people will get power-hungry enough and put the pieces together eventually. Only the most ambitious employees got sent up here. They're smart people. If we've discovered the possibilities, you can be certain they have. I hope you see why we have to stop them at all costs."

"I guess. But sunlight as a weakness — it's a bit of a gamble. What if it doesn't work?"

"That's why we need to work together one last time, partner. If this fails, if enough of them survive or it doesn't work at all and I guessed wrong, then you have to do the hardest thing. An eventuality I'm trying to avoid."

He knew what she was going to say. "The slaves. You can't be serious."

"Neither of us want innocent people to die. But it's clear that at least four have already. And the numbers in here added to the Renegade's evacuated force don't add up. There are still some missing. Maybe they transformed and died from exposure to sunlight. Or maybe someone didn't want to change, and put up too much of a fuss about being a perpetual snack. The Doc and his Initiates are already murderers, they've admitted as much, and they're not going to stop. Sometimes you have to take a few lives to save a lot more."

"So if your plan fails, if you get captured, or if you succeed but they aren't even sensitive to the sun, as a contingency I have to execute all of the regular people the Initiates are feeding on. Including myself. We're going to starve them to death."

"There's a sliver of hope that it won't be necessary. A small chance my plan will wipe them all out." She locked eyes with him then, testing his will. "But we have to be pragmatic. You should prepare yourself."

She pulled a gun from under a cushion on the couch she was sitting on, and placed it in the middle of the coffee table next to the sketch.

"You'll be needing this." She rose, and started out the door.

"Wait, what? You're going now?"

"They gather in the lounge all the time. It's the largest concentration of them — the best chance to catch them all, and one side is currently facing the sun. I'm going to give it a skylight."

"So soon? Don't we need to plan this out more?"

"It's now or never. I'm self-aware enough to know I'll lose my nerve if I think about it much longer. The opportunity is there. We need to take it. Go to the slaves. Try to smuggle in enough suits to get them through the vacuum areas to the shuttle — evacuation is obviously the preferable option. You need to get them off of this pod and back to civilization. Call the Major General from the shuttle and report. He'll know the best way to get you ground side. But if it looks like you're going to be captured, or can't get to the shuttle, if even one of the slaves tries to stay..."

She trailed off, staring at him silently, intently, until he nodded his acquiescence. Then she walked out purposefully, while his gaze never left the gun on the table.

As she strode with a brisk pace through the hallway, leaving her partner behind, the Investigator felt an overwhelming sadness weigh her down. She didn't want this responsibility, but she felt duty called her to it. And even though she wasn't that close with her partner — her isolationist personality was partially what brought her to a remote job in space in the first place — she knew that the brief, business-like encounter they just had would be their last. With a mental clarity seldom achieved, she had no doubts whether she would walk away from this final mission.

The Doc had given the Investigators pretty much free mobility around the apartment pod, until they decided whether to transform or not. A sample of his graciousness.

She got to the end of the pressurized area, donned her suit, and after the hiss of an airlock cycle, started heading quickly to where the explosives were held. She had already explored enough to know they weren't guarded. The Doc was very good at keeping his people in line, and they all had a strong desire to continue their new way of life, so there hadn't been many fights. With the exception of the unchanged people to feed upon, the Doc didn't feel a need to have designated security or post guards. His utopian society of space-fairing people was above such things.

The makeshift equipment storage room was really an old workout room. The benches and treadmills now served as shelves for spare items of every type: suits, lights, and drills were scattered about in roughly organized piles. The Investigator found the stash of explosives near the other mining equipment. The arrogance of not having these under lock and key was shocking, stupid. The Doc would learn from this mistake if he got the chance. She wanted to make sure he wouldn't have it.

She grabbed a nearby duffel bag and shoved in as many of the explosives, detonators, and timers as possible. Slinging the bag over her shoulder, she left the room quickly.

The hallways were eerily devoid of people as well as pressure. The Investigator didn't encounter anyone on her trip to the nearest external hatchway. It opened easily, and she moved into outer space.

By using the pieces of the pod itself she climbed over it much like a ladder. The blocked windows provided an advantage: there was no chance she'd be spotted outside. She stopped where the sun's photons struck the lounge, a wall of light reflecting back at her, a brief glimpse of a harsh heaven, dimmed only by the built-in tint of her visor.

She planted an array of explosives at intervals around the entire face of the section, ensuring a wide gap when they blew. She then attached a timer and set it for nine minutes. She had done some quick mental calculations and determined that was the optimal amount of time for what she needed. After a deep breath of the suit's oxygen, she started the timer.

The race back was almost as uneventful as the way out, if a bit more rushed.

Eight minutes.

She opened the hatch, pulled herself back inside.

Seven minutes.

The Investigator hurried by several of the Initiates, communicating with each other in the vacuum in a way she had still not determined.

Six minutes.

Slowing as she passed, she noticed a couple at the very beginning of zero-g foreplay, hands and eyes moving all over each other. For a fleeting moment she was jealous of their ability: to touch another person's skin in this harsh void. An event never before experienced by humans in all of history. Never before imagined possible in the future. As she came into view they dismissed her off-hand — a slight interruption to what they had planned.

Five minutes.

She found the airlock back to the pressurized section of the pod. Once inside and cycled, she kept the doors closed, tore open her suit, and pulled the rest of the supplies from the bag.

Four minutes.

She slipped a ring of explosives around her body, donning death as effortlessly as a cocktail dress.

Three.

She attached a manual detonator, which she moved to the inside of her glove, a wire strung back along her arm to the explosives.

Two.

Prepared to face her captors, she discarded the bag and sealed the suit back into place over herself, masking the added bulk.

One.

The Investigator expelled the air and moved back into the vacuum interior area. She sprinted toward the lounge, determined to see for herself if her gamble would pay off.

She got to a doorway in the back of the room precisely when the last seconds ticked over on the display.

The explosion had no audible volume — though she could feel an incredible vibration through the door frame she gripped tightly with her hand. Visually, it was a brilliant blossom of warm colors fading immediately into the bright bloom of a blinding sun staring straight through the massive hole in the wall.

A few of the fiends had been caught in the explosion, bodies now floating in fragments. The rest of the room stood still in shock for the split second it took the heat of the sunlight to register through the cloud of debris. Some flung up hands to protect their eyes and faces, while others dove toward what little shadow still covered parts of the room. For most, it was too late.

The Investigator watched as about forty of them were instantly burnt to a crisp — third degree burns covering their whole bodies. Where some grabbed at a wall or chair for purchase, skin scraped off easily, exposing muscle and bone that sizzled with as much abandon as their outsides.

It looked like they were screaming silently while they could, but the end came quickly.

The Minion appeared next to her. The right-half of his body was totally seared. His right arm now ended in a rigid black stump near the elbow, while his right eye and most of the hair on his scalp were nowhere to be found. He looked disgusting. And ferociously angry.

He pulled back his one good hand as if to strike. But then he hesitated, and his lips began moving like he was talking, but she obviously couldn't hear anything with no air for the waves to travel through. Then she decided he was either talking to himself, or someone remote, though she couldn't find any device he might be using.

The Minion stared into her soul, and she was unflinching. She had committed mass murder of the next evolution of her own species. And she was glad of it.

With his good hand, he grabbed her arm and started ushering her back to the airlock. She resisted the urge to shake him off and offered no resistance. Once they were pressurized, she pulled back the hood of her suit and waited.

"I was ready to kill you where you stood," he snarled through half a mouth. "Tear your head off with a single swipe. Then I would spend the rest of the day chewing on your frozen blood. But the Doc wants answers, and I think he'll have better ideas for a slower, more creative way for you to die."

She said nothing. Only stared back, afraid that a single word misspoken would give herself away. The Minion grunted, grabbed her again, and started shuffling forward, obviously having more trouble with his torched right leg in the artificial gravity and Earth-like pressure.

After a long, awkward walk with the Investigator refusing to aid the hobbling Minion, they arrived at a private bedroom, part of an expansive master suite. This had probably been reserved for visiting executives. And the Doc was there standing in the center of the room, apparently interrupted in the middle of feeding. Two of the female slaves were naked, proudly showcasing open wounds, lounging on the large, fancy bed behind him, one of them with blood still oozing from a breast, the other with it running down her inner thigh.

The Doc was enraged, unkempt, jaw firmly set in a small gesture against her violent defiance. "Come with me," he commanded.

They obeyed, and followed him into a large parlor, intended for entertaining guests. The room was filled with a chorus of upset voices that hushed as soon as the Doc entered with the Minion and Investigator in tow. The Investigator estimated that at least two dozen of the not-quite-human-anymore creatures were in attendance at this mock court.

The Doc motioned for them to move to the middle of the room, and sat down in a seat that had been reserved for him. "How many?" he asked, voice brimming with stress.

"From what I saw, nearly fifty," the Minion offered.

The Doc growled at the news. "So, you have discovered our greatest weakness. A flaw in the engineering I hadn't anticipated. And I must assume your partner is aware as well. You know, of course, that now we can't suffer either of you to live. It is ironic, is it not, that what started you down this path was an investigation of the first murder in space? And now you have multiplied that manyfold. Committed an atrocity so terrible and great in its consequences that you cannot begin to perceive how it alters things. Did you truly know what you were doing? Or were you simply trying to eliminate as many of us as possible?"

The Investigator met his gaze, and remained mute.

"Bring her to me."

The Minion strong-armed her closer to the Doc, and then moved back to his place near the edge of the crowd, blocking her from the doorway and only escape route.

"Your cooperation does not matter. We will feast on you until your veins are dry and brittle enough to crack under their own weight. You cannot have imagined any possibility but a slow death when you started down this road. There is something deeply masochistic about you."

After a hard stare and a long moment, she responded to him for the first time: "You and your creations are abominations. Cannibals."

The Doc chuckled. "I was considering giving you the option of begging, though it would have been fruitless. But now I'm eager not to delay your torture any longer."

In a blur of motion the Doc rose from his chair and stood face to face with her. With unbelievable strength he pinned her arms against her sides and bit sharply into her neck, sending an intense, gasping pain into her brain.

Finally, with him this close, the Investigator calmly pressed the button her thumb was resting against.

Zero.

Chapter 22: The Harbinger, and the Investigator becomes the Ace

He walked into the slave barracks with his finger on the trigger. They were all sleeping on low cots shoved closely together. The Investigator had not expected that, but then again, he hadn't adjusted to their circadian rhythm, which could be almost anything when freed from the planetary constraints of a day/night cycle.

He paced back and forth among the living food stock, his guts in a twisted mess. When his heart should be calm and holding steady there was instead an audible thump-thump crowding his thoughts. He knew he was breathing too shallowly for this sort of operation. He considered again that he was being asked to be the ultimate utilitarian: to put bullets in the brains of people as innocent as anyone could be in this screwed up situation.

Their deaths won't be frightening, he reassured himself. Just an empty continuation of their sleep. A silent passing of their consciousnesses from this universe. He could have already done the job and been gone. Even hurled the weapon into the bleakness of space, with enough momentum to send it flying forever in the frictionless medium.

The Investigator wasn't sure he *should* do it though. Wasn't sure of anything, except that he'd never convince these people of his partner's crazy plan, much less make it to the shuttle if he did. He had felt a slight shake that could have been the explosion, but he was playing the waiting game. For a moment he considered trying to be a hero, rousing the slaves and organizing a resistance, to join in glorious battle when the first of the Doc's crew burst through the door, shouting: *If we are marked to die we are now to do our country loss; and if to live, the fewer men, the greater share of honor!*

He abandoned the idea after inspecting the gun. It fired a sealed cartridge with an internal piston, meant for quietly destroying typical human flesh, not the reinforced carapace of one of the new Initiates. No, the slaves would be better off if he ended it now, quickly, painlessly.

And still there was a gossamer strand of hope he held on to. That his partner would be the one to come rushing through the door, with assurances that they were all safe, and could go home now. Or even that no one appeared, and after waiting an agonizing amount of time he could herd them all back to the shuttle and be rid of this despicable place.

He saw through his own misgivings, and the Investigator moved to the closest sleeper. It was a long-haired blond sleeping on her side, fingertips curled around the tattered edge of the meager blanket afforded her, puncture scars visible on her neck. He pointed the barrel at her temple, and prepared to squeeze off a round. With sudden clarity he knew he would turn the gun on himself when he was finished, so he didn't have to live with guilt or remorse. Despite its disturbing nature, it was a strangely calming thought, and he felt his aim steady.

At that moment a huge ear-splitting boom erupted from the direction of the corridor. The room heaved back and forth, throwing the Investigator to the ground.

As the slaves bolted upright from their unexpected wakeup call, he discretely holstered the gun. The idea that he was here to execute them probably wouldn't go over well. He was glad his brain had cleared and was working soundly once more.

"Hey, what's going on? What are you doing here?" One of the slaves at the far end of the room asked loudly.

Putting on his best ignorant face, the Investigator shrugged from his position on the floor and slowly picked himself up. "I...came for some company, but that sounded like an explosion. I'll go check and report back."

Right as he reached the door amidst words of protest, one of the Initiates walked through, bumping into him. He didn't recognize her, but she was the same pale shade he was accustomed to seeing by now. Though with her dark features, it looked more natural on her. Forgiving the couple teeth shaped like knives, he found her ravishing. His mind stuttered in the instant transition from thoughts of death to sex.

"You!" she said, eyes wide with recognition. "Quickly, come with me." She pulled on his hand and led him through a maze until they got to a closet large enough to fit into. She pushed him inside, followed, and closed the door.

His heart was running rampant again, and for many more reasons than his brain could comprehend. He knew a large part of it was fear, and that he stood no chance against this woman if it came to a fight.

"What? I didn't do anything. What is this about?"

"Your partner was a homicidal, suicidal maniac. She just slaughtered the Doc with over half his people, and killed herself in the process."

Even though he knew it had been coming, he still felt a deep pang of loss and grief to hear the news. They shared a long history, and part of him had been in denial, thinking they would both be on the shuttle home.

The chalk-white woman with silky raven hair was staring at him without compassion, but also without urgency, giving him what time he needed to accept this.

"And?" the lone Investigator eventually prompted, breaking from his revelry. "What do you want from me?"

"Without the Doc, the few remaining Initiates are in shambles. They're in disarray, trying to salvage a hierarchy and some order from the chaos. I'm going to bring them that order."

"Who *are* you? And why are we having this conversation in a cramped little closet?"

"I was the Agent, with my own agenda, which I'll explain later, but for now, know that I see a play to be made. My organization wants these people as allies. But I don't know them. They don't know me. It'll be hard for them to accept me as a leader. I need to pull an Ace from my sleeve, and I need it now. Most of the others would undoubtedly like to rip your limbs off and bathe in your blood, but I think I can make a compelling reason to keep you alive. We all know who you work for. We're going to need inside knowledge to survive what's coming and keep this movement, this adaptation, alive."

"So you're proposing that we help each other in some mutually beneficial relationship." He waited a moment for confirmation, and saw her nod. Then he continued sarcastically, "OK, you save my life right now, and in exchange all I have to do is become a traitor to myself, my country, the Company. Sure thing."

"Be serious!" she barked at him. "You're choosing death and dismemberment if you deny me now."

"How could you trust a traitor? Once I turned on them, why wouldn't I turn on you?"

"That's easy: you would have nowhere left to run. Up here, does your country exist? Do you see any borders? Any boundary-lines in space? What's left of the Company's presence? Even their power has limits. Once you turn you would have to stay up here, with us, just to keep yourself protected from retaliation."

He lost it then, stuck in this tiny room, on this insignificant pod floating in the middle of utter and complete emptiness, not under anyone's control or jurisdiction. Away from all authority. From anyone he had ever known. Alone.

He collapsed on the floor and started weeping quietly.

"I'm weak. I'll do what you want. But it's not because I believe in this adaptation like it's the next level of the human race. Our saving grace from a dying planet. That's shit. It's because I don't want to see blood spurting out of a missing arm or have an empty eye socket before I die." He sobbed a few more times, and then peered up at her, a hard look on his face. "But there's one condition. One thing I won't do."

She looked down at him with something like pity, or possibly annoyance. "Out with it then."

"I won't help you kill innocent people. No matter what the situation is, that's where I draw the line."

"It may come to that eventually."

"Then kill me now."

She pondered for a second, then offered him a hand and pulled him to his feet. "I think not. But if you defy me with *any* order I give in the future, I may kill you then. Until that time comes, I promise to keep you safe."

He laughed uneasily at her vow, getting some of the stress out, and wiped the tears from his cheeks. "I suppose that's better than getting mauled."

"You are no longer an Investigator then. You're now my Ace."

"Ace, huh? And what does that make you? The Agent still?"

"No, I'm the Harbinger. The face of things to come."

He twitched at that name, certain it was a significant omen. *An important portent.*

He was also nervous at the thought of having a new partner, especially one he couldn't keep his eyes off of. She was equal parts beauty and terror.

"So, what now? How do you declare yourself dictator and take the reins?"

"We'll do that as soon as possible. Gather the survivors and explain the situation to them. But first, in order for them to accept you, you'll have to undergo the Initiation."

With that, she started undressing.

He watched.

After she flung her shirt aside, she gave him a puzzled look. "Come on, take off your clothes."

Mouth agape, eyes wide, he struggled to form words. "Wait, why? Isn't there a pill or injection or something? Can't we do that with our clothes on?"

She laughed, sounding cheery for the first time. "I will say one thing for the Doc, he did a good job keeping his secrets. No, my Ace, the transformation spreads like a disease from one person to the next, permanently changing their genes over a very short amount of time. There's only one way to transmit it. And for that, we both need to be naked."

Misery acquaints a man with strange bedfellows, he mused.

She finished slipping out of her undergarments, and stood there before him bare in the stuffy closet. He was speechless as she suddenly kissed him fully on the mouth, felt the pressure of her breasts against his chest, and her hand tugging at his belt.

Part II
BUILD

Chapter 23: The Major General

The Major General was shaking his head at the report on his desk. First his special operative never checked in, so he presumptively, reluctantly, declared her KIA. Now this report. All this time, all this effort, wasted. He needed a good reason to get the billions in public funds required to achieve his goals — and *this* — this was exactly the opposite. There was no covering it up.

The report detailed an intercepted transmission, highlighting the fact that it had been sent to a list comprising all the active parties of the ongoing space murder investigation, including the victim's family. That meant he couldn't fake it — pretend that it said something else, or that they couldn't decode it properly. With just a little vagueness he could have woven a masterful story. But the text was strikingly clear.

This was a stark declaration that the female Investigator had gone far above the call of duty to sacrifice herself, afraid beyond reason of a free society in the stars, and in the process eradicated this strange genetic disease that somehow allowed people to limitedly survive in a vacuum. It explained the first killing and how the Doc had survived. It explained the disappearances and rumors. But there was no political force left to war against, no one left to blame but maybe the Company whose research started this mess, and they had lost enough personnel and sunk enough money into a top-secret project that wound up getting exposed and canceled to have learned a significant lesson from this venture. The remaining Investigator said he was the last one alive, and in minutes would be dead himself from wounds sustained. Getting this clarifying account of events out was his final act. It left no motivation to return to the station. No one to rescue. And there were very few questions that remained unanswered.

In short, this message wrapped up the whole thing in a neat little package.

The Major General *hated* neat little packages.

The investigation was finished. There would be no funds coming in. Perhaps the other stations would hire more guards, tighten security, establish new protocols, but that was about all that would come from this, beyond the loss of life and the temporary shutdown of a perfectly good space station with all its equipment and supplies.

The Major General was shaking his head because it still felt so wrong to him. *Utterly unbelievable.* His gut told him that even with only minutes left, the Investigator would have followed procedure and not sent a message this important to a list that included civilians and possible witnesses. The Major General kept second-guessing himself though: *Would I, as a dying man, care about such a mundane thing in my final moments?*

Reading over it again made hackles on the Major General's neck rise. Sending a message like this was almost begging him to doubt it and keep the investigation open, devoting more time and resources to what should be a closed case. It would be a career-ending move, working on a project that everyone else assumed was finished.

The Major General sighed and filed the report. Underneath it, the unused plans his Orderly had found for a battleship in space were lying there on his desk staring up at him. They were an invitation. To realize someone else's dream from the past.

Knowing these new, startling possibilities for what humans could achieve in space made it easier to have an open mind. To imagine a new future. Many different futures. Some of them quite pessimistic. And maybe...just maybe it was enough to convince the government financiers. *I can frighten them with this. Truly scare them into acting.*

He decided to make some calls. Right then and there. Get the engine of process roaring.

He'd keep one ear on the phone. And the other listening to the sky.

Chapter 24: The Renegade

He paced and paced, thinking only of how mediocre his life would be in the future. He had been one of the pioneers here in space, and he had slinked away from catastrophic glory by bringing people to this new station. Sure, he had saved lives. But he knew that they would all become incredibly average, boring lives in the days to come.

He was walking briskly back and forth, forced to turn around every few steps thanks to the small size of this station's observation room. Feet thumping against the ground in a rhythmically interrupted sequence. And like his pacing, the Renegade's thoughts were a staccato beat he seemed unable to escape.

His small band of survivors had commandeered this station when they arrived. Using threats and fear to force everyone to cooperate, or at least get out of the way. There had been a few dissenters, but the Renegade's quarrel was not with them. They were placed on house arrest, fed at regular intervals, and promptly ignored.

After explaining the situation, his crew began training and arming those who would help. The Renegade's initial plan was to use this station as a launching point for recruiting everyone else he could. He was creating a small army, and to bolster their ranks he sent emissaries to the other stations as soon as possible. The envoys met with limited success. Most people knew about the first murder, but weren't impressed by fairy tales of suitless space-walking humans. He knew this was a numbers game, and the Doc's forces were already far ahead of his three dozen engineers and scientists turned soldier.

While the Renegade was planning how to convince more people to join, he had seen the Investigator's transmission and the silence that followed. He couldn't deny it, and he didn't have any reason to assume it was fake. The ironic thing is that the simple fact of another voice claiming the same things he'd been heralding would've been just what he needed to get a bunch of people off the fence. But he didn't need them now. And that was perhaps the hardest part. He had been wetting his toe in the surface of this ocean of leadership, and now he would give it all up. The Doc was dead. His revenge had been stolen from him, and with it, his command.

The Renegade knew when he got back to Earth that he would have to face a harsh inquiry by the government and — even more frightening — the Company. But he didn't much care. At this point, he could see the future unfolding before him, transparent and banal, and without the satisfaction of seeing his former boss begging for mercy he would never receive. The volcano of hatred in his chest would sizzle and compress into a chunk of coal that he would carry with him for the rest of his life, rather than building and erupting out of him during a climactic confrontation. He had no outlet. No choice. Only a mediocre existence; planet-bound forever more to that same dull rock that billions had preceded him on.

As the depression sank in and the Renegade slowed his pacing, a subordinate stepped inside the doorway and knocked.

"Yes?" The Renegade asked, partially thankful for the interruption, while simultaneously annoyed by it.

"Something you should see." He handed the Renegade a small display. Paused on the screen was a video that was publicly viewable on the net. According to the metadata, millions of people had already watched.

The freeze-frame showed a beautiful Japanese woman against a nondescript background. A faint feeling of familiarity invaded his gut at the sight of her face, which featured a tightly drawn smile partially concealing unnaturally sharp teeth, but he couldn't consciously figure out where he knew her from. He pressed play.

"Friends," the woman in the recording began. "We made this video to let you know that whatever you may think, you are not alone. We are the first of our kind, and we have survived a cataclysm! Endured the gauntlet! And now we're here to help. You might be hiding in the dark, or have run away from what you know. Your friends and family think you lost. You feel you do not have the strength to face the future. Not even tomorrow.

"It is not as bleak as you think! We have been persecuted with explosives! And though we lost loved ones, including our greatest, the father of us all, we persist here where our first line of defense is this: those who wish to hurt us can reach us no longer. Those that are afraid of what we represent — a true evolution of the human species, true freedom — have no power in outer space. Those governments, like the one that sent a suicide bomber into our midsts, have no presence here. No bases to launch an assault from. That knowledge is how we sleep peacefully.

"We know some of you have been captured or arrested, others killed by ignorance. But today we give you hope! Not a virtual offer, not false promises. Real, physical relief. The best aid there is: a haven.

"We are an oasis from society. We are the chaos attacking your Company masters. We are the flare fired into the night sky. The lighthouse on the rocky shore.

"Join us and be free!

"Do whatever it takes: pool your resources, cash in your insurance, your shares, your retirement. Sell your car and your house — you will have no use for such things! Use any means you can to get out of Earth's orbit and live with us as you were meant to among the stars!

"You don't need a specific destination. We will find you once you start the journey. We will guide you. You will not be turned away.

"If you can't find a flight, can't charter or steal one, if you can't escape Earth, then you can still find us on the ground. We will have friends looking for you. Safe harbors against the storm. Just give us a signal. Fire your flare.

"Join us, friends, and fear no longer."

The Renegade should be terrified at this news. It implied many things: that the explosion was not as successful as the Investigator's message claimed, that the Doc's followers presumably no longer resided on the old station or apartment pod — as those were known locations — and that they had agents elsewhere. On other stations. Earth. But no, that was impossible. There was a quarantine. He couldn't believe that anyone — even genetically modified by the Doc — could survive re-entry without a ship. *Maybe there had been time. Before the quarantine.* A sliver of doubt jammed in his brain.

Seeing that the Renegade didn't have an immediate response, the subordinate offered: "Most of the people online think it's a hoax. Amateur analysis of the background and efforts to identify the woman both seem to be dead ends, and the mainstream media isn't humoring the video beyond a quick one-liner about its existence. Some even say it's a viral attempt by the space tourism agencies to drum up more business."

He couldn't quite wrap his head around all the possibilities at the moment. But the Renegade wasn't scared. He had remembered where he'd seen that woman before. She'd been on the last personnel transport to arrive at the old station. And her teeth had *not* looked like those of a demon bat, as they did now. *A byproduct of engineering? Or a rite of passage?* Why didn't matter. It was a vital clue. The brief memory of her lifted the shadow of depression looming over him. In fact, he felt a grim joy enveloping him — spreading from that once fading ember to fill his extremities with the one thing he thought had been taken from him forever: purpose.

He smiled at the subordinate as he handed the display back.

The subordinate grimaced at the sheer murderous delight on the Renegade's face.

"Call a meeting of the lieutenants," the Renegade commanded. "We have to do a sweep of every station. We don't have the troops to send an armed envoy to each one in parallel: it'll be more dangerous for us now, so we'll do one at a time. We'll get as many as we can to join us here, and we'll take as much equipment and as many supplies as we can carry. And in the process, we'll inspect everyone's teeth."

The subordinate departed, slightly confused but knowing he had been dismissed, while the Renegade kept thinking about his next steps, a cloak of dread settling on his shoulders. *Have I already been outmaneuvered?* Perhaps those changed by the Doc had become truly decentralized — living in small cells to avoid notice, blending in with the crowd on each station. Or, with their ability to survive the vacuum, maybe they were free-floating outside the stations, sneaking in only when absolutely necessary. The doubt returned: *Is it possible the Doc's mutation is already on Earth?* He would have to place spies on other stations while maintaining a central defense here. He needed to intercept as many of the new demons as possible. *I need more people to pull this off.* Then he'd interrogate some, find out what the situation was ground-side beyond what the media reported. And maybe let a few through, trail them to see where they led.

The Investigator's message had been a ruse to throw him off, keep him a step behind. Or it had been a legitimate report by a dying man trying to do the right thing with incomplete knowledge. Regardless, it was the last transmission to come from his original station. Yet, that propaganda video had gotten onto the net somehow, from somewhere. He would put people on tracing it, finding the path back to its origin.

Whether it was footwork across all the stations or electronic packets through all the nodes of the net, he would follow the trail back to those inhuman creatures, and he would destroy every last one of them.

The Renegade smiled to himself, and looked out at the stars like a biologist looking through a microscope, trying to find even a single spec out of place.

Chapter 25: The Mouse

She woke slowly to the strong smell of antiseptic. Subdued white everywhere. For a moment she thought it was a dream, but once she was fully awake she realized where she was.

A hospital. She wasn't in her own clothes. An IV was stuck in her arm.

The last thing she could recall: the Princess, holding on and not letting go. Inexplicably biting until the neighbors burst through the door, then sending herself crashing through the window.

It was a nightmare she didn't want to remember. The Mouse couldn't imagine what had driven her friend to such desperate measures. The Veteran and his club must have tortured her, driven her insane.

Anger welled up inside her. Manifesting itself in quiet tears she quickly wiped away. She had been betrayed by the one person she always trusted. And it was more than a betrayal of words — the Mouse put a hand up to her neck and gingerly felt the still tender wound that attested to her friend's violent actions.

She had been rejected before. But never physically injured by someone she had already put faith in. The idea threatened to overwhelm her, and it took all her willpower to push it down. Maybe the Princess could still be saved, their friendship mended. It would take time and work, but the Mouse was prepared for those things. She just needed an apology.

She knew the stubborn personality that bruised and bit her would not give it. It was that knowledge from which the anger grew.

At some point later — the Mouse couldn't tell the passage of time in this sterile, clockless place — a uniformed policeman walked into her room.

"I'm here to ask you some questions," he said by way of introduction, making no move to shake her hand or form any sort of contact. He kept a respectful distance from her bedside.

"Hello," she said, unable to think of anything else to say.

After a short, awkward moment, the officer cleared his throat and started rambling in monotone: "I'm sorry for what happened to you. You should know that this is far from the first case of a biting attack recently. I've been put in charge by the department to look into this alarming trend. It might be a new rabies epidemic. Although the doctors assure me the tests for you came back negative. Everyone else I've talked to so far has been surprisingly unable to help or unwilling to press charges. They all seem too embarrassed, or claim that it happened so fast they couldn't see. Others haven't been so lucky. There've been five or six deaths in the past month, all with similar wounds. Maybe it's a new strain. You should be thankful you have neighbors willing to help you out. I've already spoken with them, but they came in so late all they saw was a blur going through your window. Since you live on the third floor of the dorm, I already looked into cases of broken arms or legs here at the hospital, but there's no one that's been admitted in the right time frame. So it's up to you. Are you going to help me solve this case?"

After a brain cycle to absorb everything he said, the Mouse's mind was thoroughly attached to the anger sprouting inside her. It was growing into a forest of deadly sharp barbs and brambles. She spoke with a confidence she seldom felt: "I'll help you."

"Excellent." The officer brandished a digital notepad and pen. "First, do you know who attacked you?"

"Yes, the Princess. We've been friends for many years. And we were in a lot of the same classes this semester."

"I'll get her official designation from the school. Do you know why she'd do this?"

"I have no idea. She seemed...tired. And distant. I haven't spoken with her much recently."

"So when did this all start?"

"Well, it's stupid, but at the beginning of the semester everything was normal, and then we heard about this club the Veteran had."

"A club? Like a school club?"

She shook her head. "It was never officially endorsed."

"I see. So the Veteran was in charge of it?"

"Yeah, he selected people to join and they'd stay up all hours of the night partying. The Princess and I went to go check it out, but I never went back after the first time. She kept going, and I think that's when she started to change."

"And where do you think she is right now?"

"Probably at the Veteran's. They all sleep there during the day."

"Okay, that's enough to start. You get some rest now. The police will look into this and see if we can't find this Princess of yours and ask the Veteran what's going on."

"Thanks, but please, don't hurt her. She wasn't herself when she did this."

He smiled. "Don't worry, we'll get to the bottom of this. If it is some kind of rabies she might not have been in control of her own actions. I appreciate your cooperation."

The officer nodded to her and made a quick exit.

The Mouse was alone again, with a sick feeling that she had gotten back at her old friend with a level of vengeance undeserved.

Chapter 26: The Ace and the Harbinger

The Ace saw clearly with the eyes of an outsider the social dynamic that brought the Harbinger to power and thus spared his own life. The Doc had been a leader, certainly, but he had maintained a loose community rather than a rigid power structure. More mayor than dictator.

The Harbinger changed all that. No one was foolish enough to challenge her when she made her intentions clear. As an unchanged human she had already been a formidable assassin, subtle and reticent, whereas now she gave off a dangerous, murderous aura. She was in charge until someone else cast her out. And while a few of the surviving Initiates had mumbled about it, most were grateful for the responsibility lifted from their shoulders — having a strong leader to rely on was a comforting delusion of control.

The one who begrudged the Ace the most was the Minion. He had been there for both explosions. Seen the suffering until his last good eye melted in the heat of that second blast. And while his body healed at an astonishing rate, his skin remained scarred, and half his body was mangled beyond repair. He was blind, but always knew when the Ace was near, staring at him relentlessly with those hollow, sunken pits of charcoal.

But it was easy for the Ace to ignore him. He was still in awe of what the Initiation had accomplished. It was a total transformation. It was indescribable.

While he had a pronounced longing for the balmy sunlight he would never see again and a tendency to panic when he realized he wasn't breathing during his trips into vacuum, the Ace was easily lost in the positive changes. Visually, the world was more saturated, with sharper edges. Colors were more vivid, shapes more defined. His whole field of vision was in focus at once, a high dynamic range of wavelengths allowing him to see more than he had imagined possible. It was all he could do not to weep with joy whenever he gazed out into the twinkling sea of rainbow stars. And he cursed whatever god had not given humans this level of perception from the start.

The first time he visited the unchanged humans to feed, he noticed how sluggishly they moved. They appeared poor, clumsy creatures to his new sight, and he pitied them.

In the beginning he was reluctant to injure them, much as he had been when he walked into the room with a gun as a weapon instead of his teeth, but after a few days of not feeding he realized he had very little energy to do anything, accompanied by a ravenous hunger for nutritious, rich blood. That time, when he saw the pounding vein in his victim's neck, heard the heart pushing it close to the surface, he knew he would not have to be encouraged. And it took a good measure of self-control not to keep sucking the blood out to the point of killing the human. It was only the reminder that he could come back whenever he wanted that finally gave him the restraint to avoid draining the body dry.

Afterward, he found himself incredibly alive, almost invincible. It was an intoxicating feeling. Easy to get lost in. A dark heaven of puffy clouds wisping apart together forever combining changing fluxing in jubilant rhythm worship of entropy who the ancients called Janus ender of all beginner of all alpha and *oh my god.* A vision of the Minion penetrated the fog, body horrifically scarred by the sun, a grotesque sight that brought the Ace back down to reality, a living depressant to his blood-induced high.

He and the Harbinger had developed a casual personal relationship to go along with the formal political one. He used it to keep his thoughts from diverting to his old partner, fearful that grief would overcome him. Every cell the Harbinger touched on his skin came alive, super-sensitive to even the lightest caress. He had some experience with intense physical feelings like this being brought on by the use of drugs, but he was still unprepared for what she could do to him. It made it easy to forget.

It was after one of their ferocious, energetic couplings when the Ace stood naked, arms akimbo, and stared out one of the windows, appreciating how all the stars had a slightly different spectrum to them, each shimmering in a slightly different hue. That was something he never noticed — never *could* have noticed — before the change.

The Harbinger, lying on the bed, her head propped up by her hand with her legs still tangled in the sheets, watched him looking out the window, and whimsically asked, "Do you ever wonder what would happen to human society if an unusually intense solar flare hit? Another Carrington Event?"

He laughed without looking away from the stars. It was a small, honest laugh. "Honestly? No. The thought hadn't crossed my mind. If it did I'm sure the pessimist in me would've imagined a million doomsday scenarios. Solar flare? Nightmares!"

"It would wreak havoc everywhere. Some militaries might be hardened against it. But not all of them. Not civilian equipment. Not basic infrastructure."

"Why the apocalyptic conversation?" He said with a brief glance to her.

She rolled over onto her back, addressing him upside down. "You cleared my mind. When that happens I tend toward grandiose thoughts." The Harbinger cleared her throat. "But it is a real problem. Only a matter of time before one hits. And no one is developing solutions."

"So you want to solve a planet-wide problem? Reduce society's dependence on technology? Or make the tech invulnerable? I never took you for such a visionary."

"I know I can't save the world!" She threw a pillow at him playfully. "I want to save part of it. I want save *us.*"

He squinted at her, trying to ascertain how sincere she was. "You want us to leave Earth behind. Leave its orbit, the whole region." She was as serious and calm as the desert sun. "Leave the solar system!"

"Yes."

Yes.

Yes.

In that one word a galaxy of possibilities.

He turned to look out at the waltzing field of stars once more.

"Trying to find a new home for us out there?"

After a pause for contemplation, he mused, "Even if we could get to another star, we're still much too dependent on Earth for resources."

"In the short term. The eventual goal would be true independence."

"We still need somewhere to live in the meantime. Somewhere close but where no one expects us to be."

"True," she said. "I considered that. As soon as anyone with authority realizes the video isn't a hoax and we're still here, they'll come straight for the station and this pod. We need to relocate someplace secret, someplace safe, fast."

"You have an idea, I presume?"

She stood up and came to him, embracing him from behind, and pointed past him toward a barely visible line of darkness that obscured some of the stars. "That, I think, would do nicely."

"That's the asteroid belt," he said curiously. "There are a few stations on the larger rocks, but most of it's empty and dead."

"Mmmhmm," she confirmed smugly.

"So what do you propose? Putting some thrusters on the station and moving it there?"

"Oh no! That'd look very out of place. Instead, I think we'll find a big asteroid and hollow it out. We'll have to pressurize part of it, of course."

"You've got to be kidding. Living *inside* an *asteroid*?"

"Why not? We play to our strengths, and whoever comes looking won't expect it or detect it. The lone radar signature will be one asteroid among thousands. No orderly, metallic, human construction to give us away. It's natural camouflage."

They would take the first step on a new adventure for all humanity: actually live in space, calling home a landscape their ancestors had never dreamed of living in before.

He turned around and looked at the Harbinger standing there, smiling with the knowledge of a good idea. A plan. A foundation.

It was an exciting prospect.

He kissed and caressed her, falling into a familiar pattern of ecstasy.

And he wondered what other things no human could prophesy would befall him before this journey was over. Before Janus and his month came round again.

Chapter 27: The Major General and the Captain

"The memo said this was about an op you need me on, but it sure was sparse on the details. Enforcing a quarantine? Where exactly is it, sir?"

The Major General sighed as he looked at the Captain through the video screen. He dreaded having this conversation, but he knew it was necessary to get the man on board.

"It's...in space, Captain." He waited for that one to sink in.

"I watch the news, sir," the Captain responded nonchalantly. "But it looks like the threat was contained without us having to do anything. And there was no mention of an outbreak."

"There *was* a genetic modification on the loose — I'm not sure if it's even communicable, and if so how it's transmitted. And by all accounts it's been wiped out. But I don't believe that. I've been doing a lot of thinking and the way this ended doesn't sit right with me. It was all wrapped up in a neat little package, delivered to my door. And we both know how often that happens."

The Captain nodded.

"What we do know is that this modification made it possible for at least one man — but probably more — to survive in outer space without a suit. And that a federal Investigator gave her life to prevent its spread. Beyond that we're in the dark. Except for something I remembered from an earlier conversation: the Investigators believed the work was interrupted, incomplete. And that's when my mind started racing. What we've seen — the phenotype expression, this ability to survive in space — it's only one symptom of a genetic disease. Like AIDS relation to HIV."

"I'm...not sure I follow, sir."

"If you wanted to develop a way to modify someone's genes quickly and permanently, how would you go about it? I'm no biochemistry expert, but on a high level I think you'd start with a generalized base that let you change any gene you wanted to. Like creating an operating system on a computer to run arbitrary software instead of needing specialized hardware for every different program. Once you had that, building on top of it would be relatively easy. But getting to that point must've been a long, agonizing process. Developing a tailored mechanism to accomplish it must've taken decades and cost a fortune!"

"That sounds incredible, sir. But the Company labs in orbit, aren't they exactly the kind with enough funds and long term vision to sink the upfront costs into a project like this?"

"Quite right. So after years of research they eventually arrived at a bacteria or a virus or a nanobot that latches on to a double helix and adds or subtracts amino acids at specific locations according to their designs. In essence, they have a template that could do anything to our DNA — it's a carrier system for any payload imaginable."

"You mean we've seen a limited version? There are other adaptations, other *abilities* that could be imbued?"

The Major General could tell the man was headed in the right direction. That the same conclusions he had come to were starting to latch on. Ideas that once embedded wouldn't let go. Virtual ticks embedded in the Captain's brain.

"After arriving at the template they must've used some excruciating trial-and-error simulations to see how different payloads would express themselves. The kind of experiments that would never be allowed on Earth. They got the ability to survive in a vacuum, which is actually a combination of several abilities — things like super oxygenation and pressure regulation. Then the work got interrupted. And that leads us to where we are today. We don't know *why* the interruption happened though. It's all speculation about the Doc and his politics. If only we could look through more of the files in his lab. Get access to all its records. The unregulated freedom of space means we don't have the jurisdiction though."

"I don't think that matters, sir. Most of the money up there is defense spending anyway — all well above both our pay grades — so regardless of who it is and what their individual goals are, it still comes back to the same source. Space isn't militarized. This may have been about the Company trying to get a stronger foothold before a government does. Or it might have had simple civilian uses — by surviving in vacuum we can free up resources on the planet by allowing humans to colonize space without having to find another perfectly habitable planet."

The Major General nodded. "Maybe you're right that the source doesn't matter. The end result *is* the same. Think of the consequences! It'll be colonialism all over again: with planets and moons instead of continents and islands. Any edge an individual country or the Company could gain would be paramount. And this sort of bioengineering is unprecedented."

"So we have a theory about the ultimate why, and we know where we ended up, it's just the details in between that are unclear."

"Exactly. We'll probably never know and it's all spilled milk at this point anyway. But you know that's not enough by itself for me to plan an operation and put lives on the line."

The Major General waited patiently while the Captain mulled it over for a minute before responding. He had to come to this conclusion on his own for it to be fully effective in motivating him.

"Sir, this template — the expressions we've seen: definitely the skin, but also the eyes and lungs hardening to withstand vacuum pressures, the super oxygenation of the blood — you said they're only a few of the possibilities. What are some examples of the others they didn't get a chance to finish? Tails? Wings? Night vision?"

"And here we come to the crux of it, Captain. I can see as you enumerate each idea you're becoming progressively more certain that even the slightest possibility that this mutation still exists means it's worth every effort to stop. That we must deliver lethal force to anyone with it as soon as we can get locked and loaded. Because tails and wings and night vision don't even begin to approach what's possible. It's...it's limitless. Could they see electromagnetic waves? Even tap into electronics? Short circuit metal detectors, jam cameras, disrupt security systems? Or host a computer within their own bodies, made out of purely flesh and blood? Could they control their own metabolisms? Destroy infections within themselves just by thinking, thus making any biological or chemical weapon ineffective? Could they transfer heat fast enough to cause an explosion? With even a small subset of these abilities they would — for all intents and purposes — be sorcerers."

The Captain's breath caught in his throat.

"They'd be gods."

Chapter 28: The Renegade

In the moment before he fired his first shot, the Renegade considered the path he had chosen in life.

When he emerged from puberty he had an intense killer instinct inside him. It was something that ached to be set free. And it was for this reason he realized society had laws, had consequences. His body's longing to do violence could be pushed aside by sheer force of will in order to avoid those consequences. He had to wonder if that was the only thing that separated humans from animals: the ability to choose *not* to hurt someone.

Some boys his age relied on sports where they could continually collide with others to release their testosterone. Despite having the broad shoulders for it, and repeated recruiting attempts from coaches, he had never gone down that path. He didn't like the regiment. Being told what to do and waking up at unholy hours in the morning when his physical beast wasn't even fully awake yet wasn't his idea of fun or a good way for him to achieve release.

Others used an excess of drugs or drinking to mix the chemicals in their blood down to a sedated level. The Renegade's ambition and desire to constantly be productive, to achieve something, meant that wasn't an option for him.

Instead he used his body and hormones for what his biology hoped he would: sex, pure and simple. It was his drug, his sport, his release.

Of course, it wasn't reliable. Sex didn't follow a schedule like sports did. And he couldn't pocket some and save it for a rainy day like he could have with drugs. When he hit a dry spell, he just had to deal with it. It was in those moments, not being angry or depressed, living his well-adjusted, albeit constantly horny, teenage life, when the urge to hit something would rock him the hardest.

On the rare occasion when he broached the subject with other male friends they had begrudgingly agreed they felt something akin to what he did: a warrior-hunter trapped inside, barely held at bay during their darkest hours. But he began to wonder if the girls his age felt anything similar. If they had the same yearning in their muscles when they thought about using them to destroy. The same awareness of surrounding, constantly checking for potential threats. Any excuse to release the welling power inside. Or had gender roles been so effected by evolution that this not oft talked about desire existed in only half of the species.

He could control it, of course. Most could. And when they couldn't, outbursts were usually fleeting. If that weren't the case, civilization would never have become as safe and non-violent as it had. Maybe it would never have existed in the first place.

Then he got to college, and he fell in love for the first time.

Oh, he had thought he was in love several times before that. But this was different. New. The lust and obsession turned into something terrifyingly intimate. To know another person that thoroughly who wasn't family brought about a unique emotion for him. The only way he could describe it was romantic love. If it wasn't that, then for him it was indistinguishable from whatever love really was.

The man he loved was another bright and ambitious youth. An Adonis in bed. A leader whenever a group was formed for a project or student government. A genius when it came to science and engineering. Capable of chemical, physical, and biological inventions that would, given enough time and funding for development and marketing, become multi-billion dollar industries.

The Renegade was utterly smitten.

He had to break it off.

For he knew he was louder than the voice of violence inside him. That fundamentally, he didn't want to hurt someone. That consciously he never would, if it were ever a choice he had to make. And he also knew that this man he loved so dearly was also in control. That he would not succumb to a moment of weakness and turn abusive.

But he also knew that he wanted to have children. And there was some incredibly deep instinct that bothered him when he thought about having a son. It kept him up at night, racking his brain in those otherwise perfectly still, quiet moments, the only motion the rise and fall of the hard-lined well-muscled chest beside him.

The thought of their genes mixing troubled him, creating a son together... It took him years before he could finally construct the thought consciously, but he had known it instinctively from the beginning: he wasn't certain their son would be able to control the violence. That this future descendant would win all the internal battles necessary to become a peaceful person like the Renegade had.

It was the result of the very specific combination of his thoughts about himself, and his own worst fears about the violence inside, added to the kind of person he had fallen for. Their intelligence, their ambition, their height and biceps and triceps and calves and fists and all their traits that made them who they were — both mental and physical — would combine to create a monster. An evil genius capable of much more than simple violence. A warmonger bent on genocide. Who would change the world, which the Renegade understood required pain and suffering and sacrifice. In the same way families naturally avoid incest for fear of creating an infant with deformities, he knew this to be true.

So he had broken both their hearts. The Renegade became a bit more callous to cover how much it hurt. The man he loved became less confident, and eventually less sure of his own ideas. Billion, million dollar valuations became delusions, day dreams, pipe dreams as he continually second-guessed himself.

The Renegade faltered a few times after that. A few drunken messages. A few weekend visits where old promises were remembered on Friday and forgotten on Sunday. Whirlwind moments of happiness, scarce impressions of what could have been, passed by in blurs.

He supposed the rest of his life would be uneventful after that. A humdrum life full of possibility — within all the average, middle-class limits, of course.

He wouldn't be the boss. He'd be someone less bold, less risky. An Assistant.

As time went on and the thudding, thumping, vibrating pain dulled to a slow, quiet background echo that only amplified and came to the surface rarely, the Renegade became more optimistic. He went on a walkabout. Found himself (again). Eventually, found another love.

His Husband was still smart, still capable, charming and good to have at parties: he could blend into a crowd of complete strangers without ever needing an introduction. But there was an edge, a ruthlessness that was missing. Or he simply had a more restrained ambition that let the Renegade know he was the safer choice. It meant they would never be filthy rich or famous. But it also meant a son with his Husband would not be a terrifying genius, not a world leader, not a monster. Their progeny would be successful, but boring. At least they wouldn't be starting any wars. And he wondered if parents throughout history had felt the same instinct he had. Did they know what they were creating when Alexander or Julius Caesar or Genghis Khan were conceived? It's possible his ability to foretell his son's attributes was unique. Or a delusion. But it was also possible that those parents had known what they were doing and made the harder choice. To not be safe. To unleash a monster. To change the world.

And now his Husband was dead and monsters were real, created in part by his own hand.

The Renegade imagined sitting at home on a couch sipping a light beer and forcibly laughing at a cheesy weeknight sitcom, wistfully distracted.

What would be different if I had only made the harder choice earlier?

But his personal philosophy didn't involve regrets. He did his best with the information he had at the time. Hindsight could help prepare for the future, but there was no use harping on the past.

And now, in the present, it was finally time to let the violence inside himself reign.

Chapter 29: The Mouse becomes the Lion

The Mouse let the news play on in the background at the hospital, a failing remedy for her insomnia. She told herself that she had recuperated enough to leave, but she was much too meek to force that opinion on the nurses and doctors attending her.

When she first woke up she discovered an awful taste of bile in her mouth. As if her stomach were constantly fighting against her. Nothing she did got rid of it. She had brushed and flossed her teeth until blood soaked the sink and even the overwhelming copper flavor hadn't been enough to banish the bile.

Now she laid in bed, attached to monitors, mostly ignoring the droning voices from the television, letting them wash over her without resistance.

She tuned in to the newscast momentarily when something caught her ear.

"Today, a story that hits close to home. This morning, a few moments ago, police launched a raid on a nearby suburban campus. We have some dramatic footage captured by a bystander that was uploaded to us just now."

The Mouse sat up, wide-eyed and alert as she instantly recognized the exterior of the Veteran's house. The screen shakily showed a bright, crisp morning. She could hear the repeat of weapons fire, close but muffled, and then saw several police emerging from the house, dragging bleeding people behind them. She could see some were shouting, some were sobbing, and some were Initiates. When the latter came outside, kicking and cursing despite grave, gaping wounds, their words turned into wails as the sunlight struck them and their skin crumbled apart, burning from ghost-white to charcoal-black.

What happened in there? The Mouse thought. *It's like all the Initiates are covered in killer sunblock!*

There was more blood as chunks of charred flesh were left behind grasping handles or stairs. More and more Initiates were brought outside until suddenly there weren't any emerging. The sounds subsided and the scene became eerily absent of noise, other than the occasional stifled sob. Then the feed abruptly cut off, and after a brief blank pause, the camera went back to the studio.

While the reporter rifled on about the particulars, the Mouse's shock firmly took hold of her psyche. Outside sound was drowned out by the awareness of her beating heart pounding loud and relentless, while an inner voice grew within her. Whatever changes they had undergone — the TV claimed it was a new tropical virus — it made daylight a killer. A fact which the police ignored as they dragged the Initiates outside. And the Mouse had led the police straight to them. Straight to the Princess.

She wanted to cry, she wanted to scream. But a numbness that felt medical in its completeness prevented either. She had meant for the Princess to get scared by the police, maybe arrested. Jealousy made her want the Veteran's club smashed to a pulp. But not like this. Not with death as a consequence. *The Princess is gone,* a sinking feeling in her gut convinced her. And she was the one responsible.

The Mouse tore the IV from her wrist and the electrodes from the rest of her body. The monitor started screeching, but the Mouse didn't heed it nor did she change from the hospital slip into real clothes. She bolted from the room and sprinted down the hallway, following signs for the helipad at every turn. Eventually she found a staircase and bounded up, emerging into the coolness of a late Michigan morning. The wind bristled the hair on her arms.

The rooftop was devoid of anyone else. The Mouse moved to the nearest edge. She was breathing heavy from exertion. Nervous as she tiptoed closer, fear began to slide past her defenses and eke its way into her thoughts. To avoid losing her determination, she didn't risk a glance down, instead peering out to the horizon and the landscape before her.

The Huron river, tree-lined and slow-moving, meandered peacefully on its course. A park with a canopy so thick she couldn't see through it spread out below her. Cars drove by steadily on nearby streets. A train finished pulling into the city's only station.

She realized that although a few people might see her fall — or at the very least, the impact — most wouldn't notice. This act might disrupt the schedules of a few people, temporarily. But even in this relatively small college town most people would simply go about their lives, not knowing or caring that she was gone. Eventually, she'd be completely forgotten.

She took a final step.

And pain shot up through her leg and knee. She was on an outer landing a few feet down. Nothing broken. Maybe sprained, more likely deeply bruised.

For a brief flaring moment the physical pain was excruciating. It overwhelmed her emotions, letting nothing through. The inner voice that had been growing within her was silenced. She arrived at a moment of clarity, crystallized by a new source of agony. She realized that leaving would be the easy way out. That living with the pain and the grief and the shame, tasting bile in her mouth every minute of every day, would be a more fitting penance for her sins.

She heard sirens getting closer. And crawling to the edge, looked straight down.

The Mouse saw the first ambulances arriving from the disaster at the Veteran's. She saw several blackened, unmoving bodies being wheeled inside, unable to tell one from another. The sight morphed and channeled her guilt into a stream of hot, steaming anger. She may have betrayed her friend with words, but it was the police who had taken action. *They murdered my best friend.*

Slowly standing up, letting the pain flow through her, freely embracing it, she stared five stories down from the hospital roof, and vowed not to rest until the police had paid for their crimes. Until any surviving Initiates were safe from this threat.

To keep her memory of the Princess alive, she would help them, whether they welcomed it or not.

Even if she had to block out the sun.

Chapter 30: The Major General and the Captain

The Major General didn't leave the atmosphere if he could help it. He was paranoid about his health, and he knew there was a lot of nasty radiation in space that never made it to the surface, protected as it was by that decaying umbrella known as the atmosphere.

The local police raid on the Veteran's house destroyed his last reason to pay attention to Earthly events. His one and only lead on the ground, tagged as a person of interest, gone, thanks to some overzealous, trigger-happy yokels.

So, here he was, entering a huge low-grav dry dock. It had been requisitioned from the single ship-building facility the US maintained, previously used exclusively for shuttles and probes. He had asked the dock-workers to extend its volume, and they had complied crudely. Out-of-place titanium alloy plates made a patchwork shell easily the size of a modern 100,000 plus capacity sports stadium. The single skeleton centered amidst the steel walkways and girders would dwarf the shuttles that had come before it. The Major General felt a sense of justification in this, a *rightness* to his actions vindicated by seeing plans held together in reality by nuts and bolts.

He was building a warship.

This was the first space-faring vessel humanity had ever built that would be dedicated solely to destroying an enemy and surviving the encounter. Being near the aft of the ship, he saw how the size was necessary for the redundant systems, including two massive fusion reactors to drive ion engines — terribly inefficient in an atmosphere, but capable of achieving neck-breaking accelerations in space using only electricity. Not needing fuel eliminated one danger of fires in the ship, as well as lowering the requirements for storage, further increasing the thrust to mass ratio.

The Major General promenaded along the lower walkway, pausing every so often to admire a piece of the ship that showed a high level of completion, belying the eventual edges and curves the final shape would take. He noted how any attacker would have to punch through a double-hull: the outer layer was a hardened diamond carapace, designed to be a kinetic barrier and stop any traditional ordinance or micrometeorites from causing damage. The inner layer was a softer lead compound, there specifically as a shield against radiation, both natural and artificial.

He made it to the bow, and saw the real meat of the meal: the forward battery. To further avoid accidents of fire or explosions inside the ship, there were no traditional guns. No bullets. No ammunition to run out of. Instead, directional lasers in banks running along both the top and bottom of the vessel would be able to fire in a wide cone ahead of the ship. Like the engines, they were also powered by the fusion reactors, and would be able to fire for as long as the ship was operating, never running out nor needing to be reloaded. They would wreak havoc at the speed of light, burning through most metals in a matter of seconds, and doing more damage the longer they stayed in contact. Of course, as light, the Major General knew that the lasers wouldn't have a pushing force behind them. When they needed to move something out of the way, or when the engines were using most of the power, they did have a limited supply of missiles. Containing an explosive that was essentially TNT powdered with aluminum, they were low-tech, but would get the job done.

This was, obviously, a massively expensive venture. The supposed video hoax had unsettled only a few people, but it had compelled the Major General to action. And the video combined with his fervor had been enough to convince most of the brass that the last message from the Investigator did not contain the whole truth. They hadn't run the proposal *all* the way up the chain of command. It was still need to know. And to gain their cooperation, the Major General had accepted the role of the fall guy. He'd be the patsy if this went south. *Limited liability at its finest,* he thought.

The disappointing thing about this clandestine route — other than the nasty legalize and potential loss of his pension that lay ahead — was that what he wanted most even the Air Force needed permission for: nuclear and anti-matter missiles. The former were a tested and true way of obliterating anything. The latter were a new development with an explosive power so frightening that the public might never be informed of their existence: large asteroids and small moons could be destroyed with the amount of anti-matter he could hold in the palm of his hand. But it was a setback he could live with. Their enemies weren't real military, and no one had fought a battle in space before. He was ahead of the game simply by preparing.

The Major General completed his circuit and found the Captain staring at the partially formed ship. He didn't stop to salute, but the Major General didn't mind. This was a moment for awe, not procedure.

"She's going to be big," the Major General said by way of introduction, and stuck out his hand.

The Captain realized his lapse, and quickly took the Major General's hand with a smile. "Aye, sir. But she's no carrier," he responded.

"Maybe that'll be the next design we implement. A space carrier full of smaller, agile fighters."

The Captain smiled, "That would be a sight, sir. But as long as we're intimidating defenseless space stations, we won't need it. That day will only come if we're fighting other battleships. And that won't happen if no one finds out about this."

"Well, we may have to inform the politicians, at least before I send you out. I may be crazy enough to run up a bill without telling them, and even commandeer a couple nuclear reactors from the Navy, but the idea of launching with the potential for loss of life…even I'm not daring that without more authority. I'm banking on the fact that if the tool already exists, they'd be crazy not to use it."

"Yes, sir. I agree with you there. But why would any *other* government have to know about it? This ship's existence alone completely ignores all the United Nations treaties about not militarizing space. It would be much better politically — not to mention give us a huge tactical advantage — if no foreign power knew this were here."

"My thoughts exactly. But there's always the possibility that someone else will find out even if it's kept highly classified. That's why I haven't attached your name or anyone else's to this project until I clear it up top. Any fallout will be mine alone."

"That's most kind of you, sir. And, if I may, why did you ask me to be here, sir? The ship isn't finished yet. I also haven't figured out how you decided on my name to tap for the command position."

"To your first question, I believe that every Captain should be given a chance to make requests or changes before their ship is finalized. It's far enough along that having an eye on development that's experienced with actually living and fighting on a ship could save us quite a few headaches later on. I expect you to be helping with the construction full-time.

"As for the second, you were the obvious choice. I wanted someone who had held a command in space before, and that left very few qualified candidates, as most are too old, considering when NASA lost its funding and launch-abilities."

The Captain nodded as it all sank in. This was a dream job for him. He had been about to retire from the service, and this was an amazing way to delay the domestic life a little longer.

"Thank you, sir. I'm honored."

"Don't thank me yet, Captain. We still don't know what's waiting out there. My gut says that the Investigators didn't tell us everything they wanted to before they died. Maybe they couldn't. Either way, there is something unexpected out there. Something scores of people have already died over. I'm going to equip you and your crew to deal with it to the best of my abilities, but at the end of the day, this is still a mystery we're only beginning to unravel."

"I've been thinking about that. Sir, this ability that exists already — to be able to survive without an atmosphere — think about the tactical advantage that could give to a ship like this. No need for complex and expensive life-support systems. No more worrying about hull-breaches."

"You've hit the nail, Captain. I was going to wait to tell you, but destroying whoever is going rogue out there is only your secondary goal."

The Major General's expression went from conversational to a dark seriousness: "I want that tech, Captain. I want you to take it and then destroy or capture anyone that's been exposed to it."

The Captain made a curt nod, his upward curving lips morphing into a rigid, straight line. "If this ship looks even half as menacing finished as she does in her infancy, then you'll have it, sir."

"Good, Captain. I'll pave the road. You drive the cart. I expect weekly reports on your progress."

The Captain saluted, and the Major General returned it. He started the walk back to the shuttle bay, so he could get ground-side as soon as possible. He hated coming up here.

He stopped for a moment, sparing a glance back at the Captain, who was gingerly laying a hand on the hollow exterior of the ship.

It had been worth it.

Chapter 31: The Renegade

The muzzle flashed as he squeezed the trigger.

The lightest touch and his pistol fired fast death in bullet form. He had carelessly burned his left hand trying to support the sidearm, not realizing how much energy was lost to heat in the short barrel. Now he was blind-firing around a corner, trying to convince the group of defenders down the hallway that this fight wasn't worth their lives.

The rhythmic sonic booms speeding back his way were proof he wasn't very persuasive.

Not surprising each station simultaneously had cost him lives, but the Renegade knew his losses would have been even greater if he had spread his forces too thin. This was the last station out of about a dozen he planned to hit, given the economics of fuel and time. They had been the best prepared, hearing of the raids directly from friends on the other stations, before even the news media learned of the attacks.

The Renegade had previously thought that taking a life was a hard thing to do. It was a moral situation he had hoped he'd never have to wrestle with. But the first man he gunned down four stations ago was silent when staring into the cylinder that was his guillotine. No pleading for his life. The Renegade's breathing and pulse slowed. A surreal calm fell about the scene, inexplicable against the prior roar of the firefight. Then the Renegade pulled the trigger and the throes of death were equally quiet, leaving him with a disinterested mood when the deed was done. It had only gotten easier after that.

Now he knew that he was fighting for his life, for the life of these people following him, not just access to the station's armory, though that had been the original goal. He needed the supplies, and more importantly, the people, but convincing anyone to join his cause was a perilous endeavor at best. When word got out he was stealing all the foodstuffs, small arms, and space suits that he and his troops could fit into their shuttles, it had gotten even worse.

A round whooshed by his head as he reloaded. There was a brief pause in the firing. He tried for diplomacy one more time.

"I told you. We don't want to hurt you. Let us take the weapons and we'll leave you alone."

Silence continued, and he motioned for one of the men behind the corner with him to take a look.

It sounded like an explosive hailstorm when a half-dozen shots all fired at once. His man went down, one hole clean through his shoulder, another bullet stuck in his side. The Renegade pulled him back into safety. The man would live, but wouldn't be out of bed for weeks. This raid was quickly turning into a loss. If the Renegade didn't end it soon then the supplies he carried out wouldn't be worth what he spent getting them.

He knew the slugs he fired were specifically designed for soft, fleshy targets. They wouldn't penetrate the hull or a heavy vest, and that was exactly what one wanted for ammunition on a space station. The Renegade had been fortunate enough to find a limited supply of fragmentation grenades on one of the better-armed stations, and he motioned for someone to hand him one now.

Desperately hoping that the hull was strong enough to withstand the blast, the Renegade pulled the pin, counted twice, and tossed the explosive ball around the corner.

The shockwave in the pressurized atmosphere knocked them all down, and left a ringing in his ears. When he came to his senses, the Renegade risked a peek around the corner.

The grenade had done its work with professional care. Each of the opposition's skin and vitals had been torn apart by the flying shrapnel. The Renegade walked among the bodies, ambivalent to the death and gore, knowing he should be feeling something more.

Near the epicenter, a quarter-sized puncture was sucking air out into vacuum. He motioned for his troops to hurry. Rather than stick around to patch the hole, the Renegade intended to get what they needed and run. He'd rather race against the clock of depressurization than be ambushed by another well-armed group.

His followers moved with practiced proficiency despite the carnage around them, quickly gathering most of the important supplies from the armory that had been this station's last stand.

When they got back to the airlock, breathing heavy from the thinning air, the Renegade found a group of about a dozen people waiting for him. At first alert, then merely cautious, he recognized that none of them were armed. He would have ignored them, but they were blocking his way.

"Take us with you," one of them said. A small woman with hazel eyes.

Wary of betrayal, the Renegade asked, "Why would you want to come with us after your friends and coworkers gave up their lives trying to stop us?"

The same woman responded: "We want protection. We don't know how to fight, and it's not safe up here any longer. We need to be able to defend ourselves. You're our best chance to live through this. Maybe our only chance now that you're taking our weapons away."

The Renegade nodded, seeing the logic. But he wouldn't foolishly trust strangers.

"Take them aboard," he said to one of his soldiers, "And keep your guns on them the whole way back."

The station people were herded into one of the three shuttles the Renegade had brought to the station, filling all of its airlocks. His men finished loading the supplies, and he boarded another shuttle, telling the pilot to take them home and taking a seat next to her in the cockpit.

He closed his eyes for what seemed like only a moment, but awoke to find that several hours had passed, and they were well into their flight back.

Seeing that he was up, the pilot said, "Sir, our data mining programs have found that this station had some more up-to-date news from the net."

"Is any of it important?"

"You'll definitely want to see it, sir."

The Renegade blinked sleep from his eyes and pulled up the terminal on the dash in front of him.

Skimming the headlines was enough to give him the gist of what was going on: the political situation on Earth was quickly turning into a gigantic mess. The US — whose interests and supplies he was benefiting from the most space-side — had made a press release warning of a terrorist group raiding space stations and murdering the inhabitants. That made him gulp. Never mind the reports of police raids around the country where people dragged into the daylight died screaming. And if the raid was at night the people simply disappeared into an officially unconfirmed but nonetheless well-known blacksite in Chicago. No formal arrests or trials.

The monsters formerly led by the Doc were firmly off the mainstream radar, but the Company divisions trying to continue doing research and manufacturing in space had a real villain they could pin their quarterly losses on. And, like the Company, he had only himself to blame.

The Renegade hadn't considered that anyone on the planet would care about what went on up here, especially with how easily the billions had forgotten about the first murder in space. But that all powerful corporate money machine was giving the government orders, and that now included sending a strike-force to deal with the Renegade and his people. He didn't know exactly what that force would consist of; it was probably some marines shuttled up, but no matter what or who it was, he should probably start thinking more about his own defenses. *Si vis pacem, para bellum.*

Unsurprisingly, China was uncomfortable with any military presence in space that didn't consist of their own people. Yet instead of trying to force the US to scrap the mission, they offered nearly unconditional support in manpower and materiel.

This all pointed to one thing: they needed to complete their mission and then disperse as fast as possible, preferably before their identities were compromised any more than they already were. The Renegade had no idea how much the US knew about him specifically. He could only hope his file didn't connect him to this, at least as the ringleader. Being labeled a terrorist on the ground was far worse than dying in space.

Other regions were handling things differently. Japan was in the middle of a bloody coup, the uprising faction declaring not only belief in the lost, space-faring people, but that it also had their support as the legitimate government of the country.

Europe was wholly divided on the issue even of the existence of any terrorists or genetically engineered humans in space. Each country was stalled in its own version of the same national debate.

Africa was using this news as another excuse to do some ethnic cleansing. Anyone accused of being afraid of the daylight was swiftly dealt with by hordes of vigilantes.

And, with only the occasional tidbit to work on, the search programs had determined that there was something massive and unimaginable going on in Russia. A compound hidden in the permafrost of Siberia where the demons were being reverse-engineered and tested to the limits of their abilities, one blast of radiation in a vacuum chamber at a time. Whether the Russians had actually captured any of the modified humans or were resuming old experiments on their own people was a source of constant debate in Western media.

The Renegade kept arriving at the same conclusion after his brain parsed each new bit of information: *We need speed.*

He was finished with gathering supplies, his preparations were complete — now was the time to strike.

Only one problem: he had no idea where.

Chapter 32: The Ace and the Harbinger

The Ace wanted a smoke.

Even with his newfound stamina, this was tiresome. But not being able to smoke, that was *torture.* Constructing the new asteroid home was continuing apace, but he spent more and more hours awake, doing physical labor. And all in vacuum.

They'd lost their first unchanged human the night before. The need for drinking to compensate for their increased metabolic rates during the construction was rising steeply, taxing supplies and tempers alike. He realized with a rumble in his stomach that blood would have to be added to the list of things to ration.

The Ace would have sighed if he had the air.

Luckily, as he started climbing over the face of the asteroid for another trip to haul or dig or nail, a bright indicator flashed on his sleeve display: it was urgent to get back inside, though he didn't know why.

As he clambered toward the small pressurized section they had hollowed out already, he thought about the string of disasters they had overcome, and didn't hesitate to admit to himself that he was thankful for whatever this new one was — a *distraction* from the vacuum monotony would save his sanity.

The instant he passed through the makeshift airlock he knew something was wrong. This wasn't one of their typical minor catastrophes. The room packed with people — typically alive with voices excited by the mundane pleasure of having the air to speak — was utterly silent.

The Harbinger was sitting down, swiveling on a chair to see who entered. At the sight of him, her eyes lit up, but she shook her head. The

Ace took the message and approached no further. He leaned against a back wall, waiting.

Then she addressed the jam-packed assembly frankly: "We've lost communication with the net."

A few mumbles, and one voice rose above the others: "It's got to be something on our side. Did we lose line of sight?"

"That's what we assumed at first," the Harbinger responded. "If you don't know, we've been using a secondary relay of a shuttle that moves laterally between us and a pre-existing solar repeater station in random patterns so no one can triangulate our position here. We still have perfect coms with the shuttle, and I had those on board manually confirm with visual scopes that they're properly aligned to the repeater. It's still there, and we're still pointed at it. That means the problem is on the repeater itself. Someone there is blocking our communications channel.

"This comes at too pivotal a time," she said, standing up and pacing in front of the group. "It must have been purposeful. Things are coming to a head back on Earth. I was in communication with several well-placed... *friends* positioned both ground-side and in orbit. Since we're on the far side of the sun from Earth, this repeater is the only link for us back to the digital human civilization. I believe that somebody knows that, or at least guesses it, and the repeater went dark in order to keep valuable information from us, and further, to prevent us from using it to coordinate a response to unfolding events.

"Our fortune appears to have split down the middle. As many of you are aware, the US has gone from melting pot to boiling pot overnight. There are riots and clashes with police happening every day. The few remaining pockets of Initiates are scattered and unorganized, most still coming to grips with what they are. I haven't spoken with many of them. Just as we were cut off I was working to structure things more. That will still happen eventually, but for now our progress is taking a forced hiatus.

"What's worse is that the rumors of a secret facility in Chicago are true. I've heard a first-hand account of them: it's a total abuse of civil rights, an abomination that must be stopped. But without organization we have no means of mounting a strike force to accomplish anything there beyond getting more of our kind captured. This is where fate fails us.

"Something I have kept hidden from all of you until now," and with those words the Harbinger locked eyes with the Ace, "is that the Doc purposefully ordered some of our kind off of the station after the Investigators arrived. This is obviously how we spread to the surface, but the real secret is that not everyone's final destination was Earth. Some stayed in orbit. And at least one transferred in the vacuum from a shuttle to a station, avoiding security there. Even now, the unchanged are not thinking like us. Not considering what we're capable of. And we've exploited that from the beginning."

"The end result is that we have trustworthy spies among them. And a short time ago I learned from them that the US and China, maybe a few other countries, have joined forces to create the first warships in space."

There was an audible gasp around the room as that fact sunk in. The Ace had been completely unaware. The Harbinger was trusting a lot of vital information to her own brain. He didn't like the idea of a single point of failure — even if it was someone he was sleeping with.

"And unlike on Earth, fate smiles on us in space. I don't know how many warships are being constructed, or where they will strike first. Their most likely target is the Renegade, as he's the one most adversely affecting profits up here with all of that raiding. But regardless of where the ships are headed, we will have at least one saboteur on board each ship. Of this I have been assured."

Worried expressions turned to smirks, and stern, furrowed brows relaxed over bright eyes.

The Ace was still angry with the Harbinger. He had words in mind for her later. But he couldn't help feeling a brief lift in his mood. A slight upward pull on his spirit. The exhaustion he felt didn't seem quite so monumental during that moment.

The Harbinger continued more softly, the room straining for another piece of good news: "The end goal, of course, not being the *destruction* of the ships."

A few people looked confused, but most joined her in a broad smile.

"In the meantime, my compatriots, we have a raid of our own to plan." She had brought them back from their revelry, and the Ace wondered at her mastery of manipulation. "The repeater needs to be brought back online as quickly as possible."

The Harbinger looked around the room as she spoke, as if testing the mettle of each of them one by one: "We go to capture it by force."

Chapter 33: The Lion

The Lion had entered a wasteland. Safe as she had been in the suburbs, never venturing downtown, she had no idea it would be like this. Detroit was barren of life. Miles of abandoned buildings surrounded what was left of the cultural center: a few stadiums, bars, and casinos still catered to the city's single remaining class; those who had previously been the underbelly now ran the deserted city. They were the only ones who remained.

It had barely taken thirty minutes to get here, a shockingly fast transition from the affluent neighboring towns. And as she drove slowly up and down the one way streets, she could almost imagine what it must have been like before the economic recession and loss of industry in the area had forced hundreds of thousands to emigrate elsewhere. It would have been a lively metropolis. It might have been beautiful.

But the Lion wasn't here for the nostalgia of a city she never knew. The isolation and sparse population suited her now. She just had to find the right place.

All the skyscrapers in the heart of the city were largely made of glass or fiberglass — either would let life-stealing light through. She continued circling outward.

The smell of kebabs and gyros permeated her car. Greektown still had some life in it, she was pleased to find. But that wasn't good for her purposes.

Eventually, she came across a sepia-colored brick building on the edge of the skyline. It was slightly older than its neighbors — and at ten stories also smaller — but not out of place. The windows were regular, inlaid rectangles, and there were fire escapes outside most of them, a rusted patchwork running up and down the face of the building like a giant spiderweb. To the West for 180 degrees the land was flat dirt, with patches of grass growing intermittently. Some demolitions must have cleared out the land before the money disappeared. It gave the brick building a clear view of anyone coming from outside the city. She knew instinctually that she had found her new den.

Parking her car at the base of the structure, she got out to examine her find. Hopefully it would be sufficiently vacant.

Whatever agency or landlord owned the building had unfortunately had the financial sense to turn off the electricity, water, and heating systems. It would get deathly cold in the Michigan winters, and starting fires might set off alarms still running on batteries. She'd have to be careful to disable them all to avoid drawing attention to the location.

She had anticipated the dark, and turned on the flashlight she brought to navigate the dusty halls. With all the available labor she was hoping for she could have the place cleaned up in no time.

The Lion found several people intoxicated with one drug or another, sleeping it off during the day, already so much like the Initiates. They wouldn't be a problem.

The building's exterior architecture had completely telegraphed its interior. She began feeling some disappointment that nothing had surprised her as she made her way back to the entrance, when she noticed a door with a small, block-lettered sign that simply read: BASEMENT.

The stairway down was a drafty switchback, seemingly endless. But after several flights she came to another door. This one was metal, thick and heavy. Solid. It swung open slowly with a creak, the bones of an old man struggling to stand up. When she got through it she saw the lock still worked from the inside. It was a bomb-shelter, probably constructed during the Cold War. The remnants of already-raided supplies littered the vault, but despite the clutter it was perfect: a massive, high-roofed chamber with support beams running straight through at regular intervals. There wasn't a single window, and there must have been several tons of concrete between its ceiling and the ground floor above. With the door closed she would need ventilation to live down here, but those she was providing for would be just fine without it.

Chapter 34: The Captain and the Lawyer

The Captain was simply amazed. The news of the space-born battleship had finally gone farther up the chain, reaching the politicians. A few other superpowers found out, whether by official or clandestine means the Captain didn't know. But instead of publicly calling for heads and hearings they kept quiet on one condition: they each got their own ship. Now the public — and most importantly, shareholders — knew that there was a pending operation to restore order to space and all the stations they had invested so much in. The details of the op, including the exact nature of the space ships, had somehow managed to stay classified.

China was the first to join the Americans, and paved the way for a multi-national consortium to form around building the warships. Construction on the fourth and final ship had just completed — each was funded and named by a founding member nation. This first fleet was made up of the *Jackson, Qianlong, Murad,* and *Cromwell,* from the US, China, Turkey, and United Kingdom, respectively. The names had been chosen from each country's greatest warrior-leaders — those history told were the most well-versed in genocide and persecuting minorities — to inspire fear and dread in their enemies.

After a minimum of decorum — since their was no press corps to impress — the Captain was setting sail as the Flag Commander of the small fleet aboard the *Jackson.* He admired what human engineering was capable of when spurred to action, while humbly hoping he never had to use the full power of these vessels. In his mind, a show of force was often a more effective tool than its use. If he could get the terrorists to agree to some terms — they would have to be arrested, but some concessions could be made — then he would feel much better about the whole expedition. The higher-ups had foreseen this, and bringing along a lawyer versed in international law to facilitate negotiations had been part of the mission's mandate.

The intelligence was spotty at best. The Captain didn't know who he was fighting, or why. Yet, he remembered the orders of the Major General well: acquire the tech that allowed people to survive in space, and don't let anyone else have it. Which would be extremely difficult with three other warships right beside him. Arrayed behind his ship in a diamond formation, they looked and felt more like an escort than support. And that was probably why the other countries had agreed to this arrangement in the first place.

The *Jackson* was stuck in a tangled web, and the Captain was the only one who could see it.

Addressing the bridge crew once the last ship was out of dock and ready to embark, he said, "I can finally tell you our destination." There were cheers and whoops. He had been working with these people on every inch of the ship for months. He could tell they were elated, and he wanted to be as well, but some hesitation in his gut prevented him from fully joining in their jubilation.

"You know we're going to fight these space-based terrorists. Or pirates. Rebels. Whoever they may be, they're taking resources that belong to corporations paying taxes to the United States government, while disrupting the work and livelihoods of US citizens. Like the navies of the seas it's our job to stop them, and ensure that trade and productivity continue to flow smoothly.

"We don't know exactly where they're headquartered. But the brass had some friendlies up here knock out a communications repeater they assure me is the terrorists' only link back to civilization. You can bet they're going to want to get it back online ASAP." There were nods while the crew processed this logic for themselves and found it acceptable.

"Our assignment is to patrol the space around this repeater and protect it from anything that threatens it." He turned to the navigation officer. "The locations of all the known stations and probes have been included in our database. The repeater has been specially marked. I assume you can find it and set a course."

"Aye, sir," the officer responded.

"Good. Then get us underway at half-acceleration as soon as you have it zeroed in." At that the Captain went into his study, which was a private room adjacent to the bridge. He didn't need to be around for the minutia, and now that he had some time he wanted to absorb everything he could find about the terrorists. Starting with that video on the net the Major General had convinced him was not a hoax.

As he was getting settled into the one luxury he had shuttled up from Earth — a large, plush, intimidating leather chair that was more suited to a royal court than an office — the Lawyer walked in.

She had been a rushed addition to the crew to fill the vacancy caused by the original candidate withdrawing inexplicably at the last minute. He never properly met this replacement before they launched. But one look and he wished he had. Sensuality emanated from every inch of her milky white skin.

Her hair was the perfect level of waviness that film actresses from the 1950's had captured in its purest essence, but the blond sheen she sported was well beyond the technical limitations of that era. He knew it was dyed, although the Captain couldn't find any flaws. Only that it looked a little too perfect to be real.

She didn't dress much like a lawyer: in a smart blazer and tight skirt, her clothes pushed against the boundary of professional. But technically, as a civilian, he didn't have the authority to tell her to dress otherwise.

And those lips, so full of promise. No hint of the swell caused by injections. A cartoon red bringing out their texture. He could almost feel the pressure of her lips against his. Could imagine how she tasted: an exotic candy a moment after unwrapping. A gentle tartness to balance out the inevitable sweet overdose. Glossy with a hint of moisture. He envisioned her lips wrapped around him, bright innocent eyes gazing up at him longingly, asking begging demanding that he share with her wanting his release more than he did himself lost as he was in the sight of this idyllic creature paying attention only to him his desires his basest needs lost in wrapping and unwrapping wrapping unwrapping and the surprise of her tongue—

He was distracted enough to miss her first sentence. That made him uncomfortable. Although it would be worrying for a crew member to do this to him, as a lawyer — and one on his side — he admitted it was an excellent quality.

He still had no qualms about throwing her off balance while they were in private.

"I'm sorry," the Captain interrupted her, "but I was catching up on some ship business. Could you repeat that?"

"Oh, dear me," she said, a little too sweetly. "I'm sorry. I can come back." And she started walking out.

"No, please stay." He offered her the much less imposing chair across from him.

"Well," she started, settling into the chair, making a point of crossing her legs and leaning forward suggestively. "I want to go over the basics of what your plan is so I know where I fit in." She paused. The Captain met her eyes. "For instance," she continued, "Am I just for show? To make them think they have a guaranteed legal status, when in fact you're planning to execute all of them the first chance you get?"

"What? No. That's not the case."

"Then what is?"

The Captain leaned back and slid into the same spiel he'd been given. "Considering who was up here when all this started, chances are that every one of these terrorists is either a citizen of the US or one of this fleet's constituent countries. Despite the fact that space isn't controlled or claimed by anyone, I've still been instructed to respect the citizenships of everyone we encounter. For the US that means a full jury trial, if it comes to that. Unless war is declared, which no one on the ground wants to do, because it legitimizes the terrorists."

"Hmm, thank you. Very enlightening. It's helpful to know as much as I can beforehand."

"And it's helpful for me to know the people I work with. It is a small ship after all." Emboldened by her easygoing countenance, the Captain ventured, "So while we're getting to know each other, can you tell me which country you're actually from?"

"That doesn't matter, now, does it?" She rebuffed him expertly. "You know I'm here in an international capacity."

"Umm," he stated awkwardly, not knowing how to continue, or how to end the conversation with a civilian he couldn't simply dismiss. "Unless there's anything else?"

"One more thing actually. A...*curiosity*." The Lawyer said the word like it rarely passed her lips, a seldom encountered extravagance. She made a sweeping gesture of the walls. "Why are there no windows? The shuttle I took up here had them, so I assume it has nothing to do with protecting against the perils of outer space."

The Captain perked up, knowing he could confidently answer this one. "Windows are nice for putting civilian passengers at ease, but they're a potential structural weakness, one an enemy could exploit. We use micro-cameras embedded in the hull instead. Shuttles aren't meant to go into battle, but this ship is. We take every advantage we can get."

"Ahhh," she murmured, almost moaning. "So do I, Captain. So do I."

At that, she stood up quickly, strolled to the door and stopped. Keeping one hand on the frame she turned her upper body back to him, tossing her hair aside in the process. "If I have any more questions, I'll let you know."

A long stride carried her out, but not before the Captain caught a glimpse of a devilish smile. The kind he knew he'd remember. A smile behind which he was certain so much more was waiting.

Chapter 35: The Harbinger and the Ace

The repeater station was the easiest conquest imaginable.

It had to be populated. Early versions weren't and when the networking infrastructure went down for any reason — a component failure, a micrometeorite impact on a dish — the repeater would be offline until a repair crew shuttled over to it, which could take days. So a full station was eventually built, complete with all the amenities needed for human survival in space: living quarters, an extensive gym, entertainment suites, a mess hall. But of course things didn't go wrong that often, so the crew had to have other jobs to be worth their pay. Labs were added. Huge racks of servers for processing astronomical data were included. Scientists and programmers with a variety of specialties arrived.

Generally, that meant the people on the station had careers, families. Investments both monetary and emotional back on Earth. People with simply too much to lose to put up a fight.

So it came as no surprise to the Harbinger that they surrendered as soon as they realized what was going on. There was not a single loss on either side, though one of the more stubborn scientists had suffered a severely broken arm. She allowed some of them to stay to continue their work and keep things running smoothly, as well as function as a nutrient source for the small peace-keeping force she was leaving behind.

That force included the Ace. She put him in charge, a fact which made many of the others envious. But he didn't appreciate it.

"What am I going to do here?" he asked as she was about to enter the airlock and board the shuttle.

"We've been over this. Keep everyone in line. Monitor the crew's activities. Make sure no one tries to access the parameters for the new direct beam we have communicating with the asteroid. We don't want any of them to get any idea where it is. And not having to rely on using a randomly moving shuttle as a proxy frees up that ship for other activities."

"Yes, yes, I know all that. But what am I going to *do*? You're answering a question I'm not asking."

She knew what he meant. It was obvious as soon as she mentioned these new orders to him. He was really asking, *What am I going to do without you?* But he knew her well enough that he didn't ask it outright. Another sign that she couldn't keep a distraction like him around anymore. Her thoughts were flooded by him: his long, limber limbs, his mouth, saying, doing all the right things. They were getting too close. She recalled a flurry of nights turning into days into nights without leaving the bed and how they whispered their true names to each other, that lovers' act of ultimate trust.

The Harbinger shook herself from the reminiscence. Things were too critical for her not to be completely focused. *How do I tell him that without hurting him?* This seemed the best way.

She gave him a sad smile, a gossamer thing gone in a flash, reserved for so long and then spent so quickly that the Ace wasn't sure it ever happened.

When the foot traffic moving to and fro around them briefly halted and they were blessedly alone in the hallway, she gave into the longing in his eyes and her heart and kissed him full on the lips one last time. She savored his taste and his scent and held on for a bit too long, an indulgence on her part since she intended not to see him again until all of space was safe for their people and she knew that could be an enormous amount of time.

When the Harbinger finally pulled away the Ace's eyes were still closed, reveling in the kiss. She watched him standing there, so perfect, a loving man in a frozen moment, before conceding to herself that she must go.

"You'll be fine," she uttered to his already lonely face as she turned and walked into the airlock without looking back.

Chapter 36: The Renegade

The Renegade's boots landed hard on the polymer surface of his old station. He was taking point for a group of his commandos as they jumped through the airlock and onto the once bustling city in space.

It was a ghost town.

His head was constantly swiveling back and forth, left then right, eyes on the lookout for even a hint of movement. The Renegade was on edge. He felt a heavy weariness strapped to his back like an oxygen tank. Breathing recycled air for all these long, lonely months had taken a physical toll. And mercilessly stealing from those who couldn't defend themselves, all the while transforming scientists into warriors, had demanded a harsh mental price.

Now here he was, back at his original home in space, and it felt completely foreign. He'd known when he left that when he came back it wouldn't be the same. But the contrast was far starker than he'd anticipated. He thought with sudden clarity that a place was both a location *and* a time: *If you don't grow together then you'll grow apart.* Even if the hallways weren't tomb-silent and still as pond water, even if they someday returned to the full hustle and bustle he had been accustomed to, even then he knew he no longer belonged here.

It was a sad, sobering epiphany; his life shifted phases and he didn't notice the transition. But as that realization dawned on him he recognized that everyone else had moved on from this place too. They would find every nook and cranny as empty as it looked now. There was nothing here.

What few remaining civilians there were had been shipped back to Earth, probably still undergoing debriefing and quarantine as the officials tried to determine exactly what happened. A fool's errand.

The Doc's gang had moved on and never returned. Would there be any clues left in their wake? Probably not. But this station still had oxygen, power, all the facilities and luxuries one could hope for in space, with the added benefit of no expected visitors. Plus all the working technical equipment. And he knew the others were communicating across the vast distances of vacuum somehow.

Thus a plan formed in the Renegade's head, one that might not have if he hadn't set foot back here, in this place haunted by his many memories. The highest highs. And the lowest lows his mind still struggled to pull from their murky depths.

Turning to his crew, he ordered, "We stay here. Everyone gets quarters near each other. We'll set up monitoring alert programs to detect incoming vessels. And someone remains on watch at the airlocks at all times, just in case we miss something."

The others nodded, but he could tell they felt he was wasting time. Twiddling thumbs while a fight was brewing. So he did what he could to motivate them. To keep this ragtag group of fighters together, when they were so loose a band to begin with.

"We won't sit here waiting for something to happen. We're going to rest and train and learn everything we can. Then we'll seize the first opportunity to strike."

The Renegade paused, gauging their interest. He held each of their eyes in turn, trying to force a confidence he didn't feel.

"We *will* find them. Everyone who disrupted our lives, brought conflict when we only wanted peace. Everyone touched by this genetic plague. The Infected."

It wasn't enough. He needed more.

When he continued speaking it was with an intensity summoned from his twisted insides. Rage filled guts. Bones bruised by hate. Lungs aflame, spewing vitriol.

"And we will kill them all!"

Part III
BATTLE

Chapter 37: The Captain and the Lawyer

The Captain knew something was wrong immediately.

He was in his cabin, soft synthetic sheets mixed up in his naked legs. He vaguely remembered the Lawyer coming in the previous night after his duty shift ended. She had been slightly coy, slightly playful, but obvious in her intentions nonetheless.

As he sat up and put his feet on the floor, rubbing the sleep out of his eyes, the rest of the night came rushing back. After entering she had stood by his desk, acting perfectly at ease. She began spouting a practiced monologue. He didn't hear a word she said. While she talked, he approached her and put his hands on her hips, noticing how her tiny waist was dwarfed by his palms. He then used his leverage to twist her around so she was facing away from him. He pressed himself against her from behind and started kissing her long, exposed neck. With the shear mini-skirt she was wearing he could feel every curve of her body rubbing up against him. His hands slowly slid down to the bare part of her thighs, caressing them while her gasp of surprise at his forcefulness turned into a soft moan. She reached back and grabbed his hair, pulling him in even closer. His hands were now moving up and down, every inch of her body soft and supple to his touch. And just as she seemed to be fully enjoying herself, he pushed her down so she was fully bent over his desk. She teased him, egging him on. He hiked up her skirt, planted his feet, and grabbed her hips.

He had been careful. She had been too strong, too cold, but mostly, too willing. He'd never had a woman of her caliber show this kind of interest. Or *anyone* show *any* interest this quickly. He never said or did the right thing to move at this lightning first-night pace. All of his natural tendencies were wrong when it came to romance. So he had been extra cautious with protection, but subtle enough to avoid her notice.

And now here he was only an hour or two later and she was already gone. It wasn't a lot to go on, but his intuition said it was enough. And his battle instincts were leagues ahead of his dating abilities.

He trusted his crew, but men did crazy things for hot women. And he didn't trust her or her claim that during their week of flying he'd been the only one on the receiving end of her attention. So he jumped into his uniform as quickly as possible, and made a point of attaching his sidearm, safety off.

He stopped by the marine barracks first. There, certain that he'd need the backup, he woke up half a dozen off duty marines. He had to assume the Lawyer wouldn't be alone; she had help, and whoever it was would be awake and with her right now. Then he led his small, sleepy squad to the armory and distributed rifles. The marines looked worried as they checked and loaded their weapons — they hadn't actually engaged the enemy yet and the Captain only had terse responses to their queries. He tried to assure them that it was all just a precaution, and as they neared their destination the questions and small talk died away.

They arrived at the bridge.

There she was, in all her beautiful glory, scarcely covered by a form-fitting curve-tracing sapphire dress the length of a mini-skirt, along with four of his crew — every one of them young and male and foolish and trying to stand closer to her than the others.

Despite his earlier suspicions being confirmed before his very eyes, he had to force himself to remain stalwart, to avoid the lust and jealousy her proximity invited.

The Lawyer and her men — for he no longer considered them his own — were all pouring over one of the central display consoles. She turned away from it when she heard the Captain enter and her surprise was palpable. He felt an unexpected surge of delight at the small victory of being able to break through her mask of composure.

"Captain, I…didn't expect to see you *up* so soon," she said, pointedly directing her gaze to his crotch while turning her mouth's unconscious O of surprise into a deliberate lip-biting ogle. "Are you feeling quite yourself?"

He puzzled over her odd phrasing, but tried not to let himself get distracted by it or by the memories her lip-biting conjured. He was mildly successful. "I'm fine. But what does a Lawyer need with my bridge crew at this hour?"

"I came her in the middle of the night because I felt an uncontrollable urge to go *deeper.* These exceptional young men were gracious enough to set me up with an extended analysis of our present situation. I'm merely eager to help in any way I can, to do anything you ask. *Anything.*"

While happy to interrupt before her plans came to fruition, he was still on edge, not knowing what she was capable of or what influence she had over the men beside her. "Step away from the console."

She did. Slowly. Languidly.

She sauntered toward him briefly before halting at another station, leaning against it with her back arched at the perfect angle to remind him of their time a few hours ago. To suggest that it could happen again. Right here. Right now.

His brain was losing the war among his organs for the use of his blood.

"Please Captain, it was harmless research. I can't help myself. I find this whole experience so *exciting.*" Her voice started silky smooth and finished in a husky rasp, moving through octaves like dolphins jumping in and out of water. The ultimate compliment to her body's pose.

They locked eyes and stared silently for a long, tense minute. He forgot to breathe. In her he saw rapturous futures of bliss. Infinite orgasms, each better than the last. Excitement. Youth. Temptation.

The outfit. The makeup. Her choice of words. It was all suddenly too much. Her constant, almost comic sexual demeanor had gone too far and descended into crudeness. He saw, for the first time, her act laid bare.

Her grip on him loosened. Finally he could think clearly. And thinking, act.

He ordered the marines to push the others back. They were deadly serious as they motioned with their rifles and the four crewmen stepped away. Instead of asking for another empty explanation the Captain walked over to the console to see with his own eyes the only real evidence that existed here. Doing so made him pass uncomfortably close to the Lawyer. His nostrils flared as her exhilarating scent threatened to revert all his progress, summoning unbidden a daydream of the two of them romping back in his quarters. The idea spurred unconscious action. He started reaching for her hand, to guide her out of the crowded room and into privacy. Desire consumed him as he fought to still himself. He almost succumbed. Almost.

The console was a tactical display not of the stations in this part of space, nor of the repeater they were approaching: it was the formation of this small fleet. With several simulations showing how by killing its speed the *Jackson* could instantly drop behind to get the other ships locked in its sights. It looked like she also had contingency plans for only targeting one or two of the others. And the firing solutions were optimized to keep the use of ordinance to a minimum. She wanted to save more for later.

His resolve hardened. Training took over, transforming his posture into a taut combat stance. The last shackles binding him to the Lawyer slipped off, spent and broken.

While he was still looking at the screen he heard her speak as she approached him from behind, using her lilting voice as a bellwether.

"Captain, it was an innocent thought exercise. An experiment. Don't you like *experimenting*? I was testing to see if your crew was prepared in case one of the other countries betrayed us."

Head down, monotone, he responded: "The one thing that can unite humans together, despite being economic or political enemies, is a common foe. It's not the other countries we have to worry about."

He turned to face her.

"It's you."

In an instant her guise vanished, all pretense dropping away from her face and body in a waterfall of muscle movements. Her mouth opened in a hiss, exposing fangs. *I should have noticed those earlier.* He involuntarily shuddered, remembering those bladed teeth wrapped around him. Her hands came up, reaching out, looking like they might strangle him or tear into his eyes as she leaped at him, faster than should be possible.

His hand was already pulling the pistol from its holster as he pivoted, raising it in a pirouette as time slowed and she flew in the air toward him. He had a split second to contemplate the fact that all the previous times he had taken a life it had been from a vast distance, dropping bombs or launching missiles from hundreds or thousands of miles away.

Then he fired point blank into her forehead.

Chapter 38: The Lion and the Cub

The Lion paced the length of the basement vault, ticking off a mental checklist to the whir of the fans blowing fresh air in from the outside. *We can't close the vault door until we have the new carbon dioxide scrubbers installed and the old air filtration system up and running.* That was priority number one: not being able to close the massive door without every normal person inside eventually suffocating on stale air was a huge security risk.

As she looked around, she realized the Initiates only made up half the population of the Enclave she had put together. They hadn't determined the most efficient ratio yet, but in order for the Initiates to survive they needed a fair amount of blood. *Can an Initiate survive on a single person if we time the feedings correctly?* If the subject were allowed to recuperate sufficiently they might be able to survive indefinitely. Although the Initiates seemed woefully unable — or unwilling — to control their appetites that much.

The core group, the oldest members of the Enclave, were the surviving Initiates she managed to find after the disaster at the Veteran's. The Princess was gone, the Veteran was gone, but a few had been lucky enough to be away from the house when the raid happened. The Lion was certain she now had all of them accounted for.

After that initial spurt, growing their numbers was much more difficult. It was easier to simply capture someone and keep them around than it was to persuade them in the first place. She had wanted everyone to come willingly, and although drugs or money, an alternative lifestyle or sheer curiosity had been enough for some, they still needed more. It was a fact she reluctantly accepted. She did the best she could with what she had.

The Lion had originally hoped that she could shirk the mantle of leadership and responsibility, transferring it before it became too heavy for her shoulders to bear. That these problems would be *someone else's problems.* She still wanted vengeance against the police, and to help the Initiates survive, but the thought of being in charge had never occurred to her. She had never done anything like this before! And yet as time passed people kept coming to her with questions. Expecting her to make the biggest, hardest decisions. She fell into the role of something like a mayor for this tiny city occupying a single building, without ever meaning to.

And it was *intoxicating.*

She was free of authority. Not constrained by a schedule. There weren't any parents or teachers looking over her shoulder. For the first time in her life she was in control of every aspect of how she spent her time, and there were no expectations about who she was or how she behaved.

It allowed her to be more honest with herself. About what she wanted. About the rush of hot feelings the Princess had let loose when she kissed her on the neck that night. Remembering soft, moist lips pressed against her skin—

A voice from behind interrupted her thinking. It took her a moment to realize the words were "We're ready for you up top." And that they had been spoken by the Cub, her special project. A protege. A boy who thought of himself as a girl, as ready for adventure and freedom and throwing inhibitions to the wind as the Lion was now. Still far too fragile, but that also meant highly corruptible.

"Lead the way then."

The Lion followed, beginning the long climbing ascent, and she noticed the way the Cub's hips moved up and down rhythmically on the stairs. As instructed, the Cub was wearing tight leather black pants, polished to shimmer, and large heals that she clearly wasn't used to. And like a good apprentice she had learned not to complain where the Lion could hear.

Shafts of light lit the Cub in strobing frames, highlighting every curve and curiosity normally hidden to public prying eyes. The Lion was almost overcome with desire in that moment, but she clamped down on the feeling. *Soon.* This one last item and then she could relax for the day.

They finally emerged on the roof, where several rows of shining solar panels greeted them.

"What do you think?" The Cub sounded eager to earn her approval. *As she should.*

"They certainly look impressive. But...do they work?" The panels had been scrounged from nearby houses and laboriously dragged up the many flights of stairs. Some bore obvious dents and scratches from that journey, others had scars older still.

"We tested all of them, and some are in better shape than others, but all the ones connected have been verified to work, at least to some extent. We've got everything wired and we're ready to connect the array to the building, we're just not sure we should do it yet."

The Lion could guess why. "The power grid."

The Cub nodded. "If there's any connection that we didn't cut then the power company will know we're here immediately. We'll be a new, significant source on their lines, and that's not something they can ignore."

"We can handle some maintenance people." The Lion was thinking of all the other power generators already active around the crumbling city — other solar panels, small windmills, even kinetic bicycles.

"The problem is we'll be orders of magnitude brighter than anything else. I think they'll send more than one small crew out."

The Lion was growing impatient with reasons not to do this. "Is there anything else?"

"We don't have a battery backup yet. At night we'll lose power. Even a particularly strong storm during the day could cripple us."

The Lion looked up into the sky, thinking back to all those glorious storms she had enjoyed as a child, protected behind safety-glass windows while gray-green clouds swirled in maelstrom dances and threw out hail like party favors. And she wondered if she could turn this problem into an opportunity. They still needed more people, more Initiates. The Enclave needed numbers, period. If this drew them in, then it was perfect. She was a spider and this building was her web, the solar panels a honey-sweet treat in the middle.

A smile spread across her face. It was her first trap, and she was eager to spring it. "Turn it on."

And with that last bit of responsibility finished, she realized she wanted what she had forestalled earlier even more intensely. Her anticipation rising, she leered at the Cub, "Wrap this up quickly. When you're done here I want you to come down to my Dungeon." She started walking back to the staircase, but after a moment made another decision mid-stride, and called over her shoulder as she continued walking, "And bring one of the new boys. I want someone young. And fresh." The Cub nodded, even though the Lion couldn't see her, and set to finishing her work.

The Lion was so excited that she was bounding down multiple stairs at a time. When she finally got back to the ground floor she entered her chambers, what might have been an interior office or small boardroom when the building was still being used for whatever its original intention was.

Her key turned the heavy deadbolt with a satisfying click and she pushed open the door to reveal a windowless space, the walls covered in obsidian and crimson and deep tyrian curtains and blankets. No sound escaped this muffled room. No outside light would ever penetrate this place. It was lit instead with chemical sticks and flashlights, their bright white glass covered with gels of various overlapping shades of scarlet.

There were cushions and mats in one corner, a plush area rarely used except for reclining afterward, sipping on some too-hot drink or smoking a hookah. She barely glanced that way.

Instead, her focus was on taking in the rest of the room, which was dominated by a bench, a swaying ceiling-mounted chair, and a wall with multiple sets of chains bound to it, each ending in a leather handcuff.

She slowly caressed a bull whip mounted on the wall — it was the real thing, not just for show, capable of drawing blood easily.

Moving through the ruins of the city and discovering the scraps and junk of the prior lives of its old inhabitants had been a joyous time for the Lion. Her awakening that started on that hospital rooftop had continued as she pillaged the unpopulated neighborhoods and found items that surprised and startled her in new ways, leaving a delightful yet unfamiliar feeling in her lower abdomen that she couldn't quite describe. She had painstakingly put this collection together, and grown quite fond of it.

Some of the tools in this room made her feel powerful. Made her more than a frail, young woman, helpless in the face of new and hidden dangers. More than masculine or feminine. Closer to the Initiates and their enviable ability for sudden, unexpected violence. Someone who wouldn't have shied away from the Princess or cowered before the Veteran. But also someone who would have no regrets if she did.

With these talismans she was now someone who could exact vengeance without remorse. And that's exactly who she needed to be.

In its aimless wanderings her hand finally found a harness of steel-studded synthetic material, its slick sable belt almost jumping into her grasp. She could feel how badly the item wanted to be used.

A knock on the door caused her to turn as she pulled the harness from the wall, her fond smile from remembering past experiences morphing into her stage face of sternness in the process.

She greeted the newcomers in all seriousness: "Welcome to my Dungeon."

Chapter 39: The Renegade

"We have hard seal!" one of the crew members cried out. The Renegade couldn't see who made the declaration, shoved as he was into a tight press of bodies. He had insisted on being here in the vanguard, but no amount of arguing or ordering was going to let him be the first out the door. The others were stupidly protective of him. He didn't quite understand why.

His search ideas had born fruit quickly: triangulating the position of the relay station had been almost trivial once they knew what to look for. Considering how paranoid the self-styled Initiates had been about masking their trail, staying in a Lagrange point was sloppy. Maybe the new leadership wasn't as competent as the Doc had been. Or it was a trap. Or they didn't realize the extent of the electromagnetic profile a place like this put out. Or they didn't care.

Who was going to come for them halfway around the sun?

Well, from what the Renegade could tell, *everyone.*

The governments of Earth were not about to let an unknown force sit idly atop their gravity well, protestations of peace aside. They had constructed some kind of new, enormous spacecraft, and long range scans showed several headed this way. Even to the Renegade's untrained eye the ships looked geared for war.

His plan changed with this new information from one of subtle reconnaissance and an eventual precision strike to a simple, brutish smash and grab. They had to get in and out quickly, or risk a confrontation in this increasingly crowded region. He didn't want that. None of them did.

So here he was, watching the wheel on the airlock door spin slowly counter-clockwise, metal groaning and creaking as the pressures surrounding it equalized.

He used the dreadfully drawn-out moment to worry about the team he sent on EVA to drill a hole in the hull and come at whoever was inside from a totally different direction. But he had ordered radio silence for the duration of this mission, so he had to trust they'd get the job done. It was a singularly hard thing, giving up his command and authority to an independent entity. They could wait outside and return to the shuttle after he left, then fly away scot-free. It was the safer choice, and part of him wouldn't blame them for the betrayal.

He shook off this fear like he did all the others — tiny dust motes brushed from his sleeve. They would meet in the middle of the relay in this ultimate gamble. His group's cracks would not turn into crevasses. He had brought everyone; this mission was a single point of failure. He had to trust they would all succeed, whether he was personally leading each team or not. The alternative was submitting to the stress and pressure and shear outrageousness of the situation and the fact that an earlier version of himself would be stuck shriveled in a corner going insane at the prospect of what he now attempted and the allure to give up quit and *run* was fierce and palpitating and he knew if he trembled or hesitated it would overwhelm him and he would crumble under the sledgehammer blows of his own doubt.

"We're in."

The airlock pushed open at an exaggerated, agonizing crawl, and the Renegade had a brief cry of thanks inside his own head for the fact that their earlier scans had proven accurate: there was still breathable atmosphere inside. They wouldn't have had enough air in the tanks to attempt this without it, and unlike the vests they now wore, pressure suits were not bulletproof. A small victory before ever engaging the enemy. It also implied that there were still people here. Perhaps the original maintenance team, allowed to live in exchange for keeping the station running smoothly.

The power had been cut. As they moved out into the hallway extending from the airlock he noticed that there wasn't a single source of artificial or natural light. All the windows had been painstakingly sealed. *To prevent starlight?* Even the emergency lighting systems were off. It might have been psychological warfare. The effect *was* haunting. The sole source of light was their shuttle's interior leaking in through the airlock. It was backlighting them, creating perfect targets.

"Everyone, night vision on. And last one out shut that hatch!" They each already wore what civilians would mistake for one-size-fits-all generic wraparound sunglasses, complete with earbud speaker/communicators. But these glasses were more than consumer entertainment devices: they were the spoils of a siege on a military tech development station. They had heavily integrated electronics, and flipping from normal visible light to infrared or to green-tinted night vision or overlaying a map with team indicators was a simple push of a button.

Edges gained sudden clarity, and electrons moving along wires below the surface panels gave off a faint glow. So the power hadn't been cut after all. The lights must have been systematically disabled. It spoke of preparation, which made him extra wary: *Why weren't we ambushed at the airlock?* It was a natural choke point.

They cautiously made their way forward in the murky blackness now outlined in emerald by their glasses. Guns out, safeties off. Assaulting the other stations to build up supplies had prepared them for this somewhat, but not knowing what sorts of modified people they might find, what claws and wings and poisons they might have, what they were capable of, what all fanatic extremists were capable of, while simultaneously navigating a dark maze made this mission more tense and fraught and dangerous than all the others combined. It would take an arduous effort to rendezvous with the other squad if there could be threats hiding behind every twist and turn.

The whirring ventilation system produced a slight, consistent breeze.

The Renegade was sweating.

His glasses blocked the beads from his eyes but he could feel the cool droplets acutely. Each one a source of sensation on his skin, drawing his attention to the minutia of his own body. His fingers became slick with sweat, but he was afraid to take his hand off the grip of the gun to wipe them.

The Renegade saw the squad's point person round a corner, then heard a muffled gargle. He rushed ahead, his stomach churning as he instinctively knew something had gone horribly, horribly wrong. *I'm not ready for this. Dulce bellum inexpertis.*

In the cramped corridor he sprinted around the bend and found his comrade, already still in a growing pool of his own blood. His throat had been jaggedly slashed open, the blood appearing bright in the Renegade's night vision, a searing iron-hot white against the cool ebony floor. He didn't bother checking for vitals. It was too late.

And he realized why they hadn't been attacked yet. This was not another paramilitary group like his own. They weren't going to be fighting with weapons or staging large battles. The enemy would operate like a predatory hunter, picking off his people one at a time.

He wasn't going to let that happen.

Switching from a single file patrol line to a broad assault formation, the Renegade moved them forward gradually, deliberately, with as many people near the front as the hallways could hold. He did a fast head check around each new corner, into each room they needed to clear. *There!* A shadow, too dark, too irregular given the rectangular contents of a small room with a cot and shelving.

He pulled out a flash grenade. It was attuned to a frequency his glasses blocked natively. He could watch it go off without the temporary blindness, headache, and confusion that accompanied the small explosion for anyone not protected. He threw it into the room and then took a half-step out of cover, raising his gun to look down its sights.

The dazzling detonation caught the shadow off-guard. The Renegade could see it clearly now: a man, no, something more, pale and lithe and oozing a sensual kind of danger from every pore. It hissed, instinctively raising a hand to block its eyes from the blast, allowing the Renegade to see two incisors, too long, too sharp. The frightening fangs made him pause for a split second in horror at the grotesque changes in humanity he and his Husband and the Doc had wrought.

The shock passed quickly, fast enough that the creature hadn't begun to recover when the Renegade finally squeezed the trigger and his submachine gun pumped out a burst of bullets into the freak.

It shrieked, a horrible, soul-wrenching noise, and writhed in pain. The Renegade walked forward to stand over it and shoot another burst directly into its skull. The howling stopped.

Out in the hallway he heard shouts and more gunfire. The other monsters must have heard this and come running. He about-faced and jumped into the action. They were surrounded in this narrow section of the station, attackers coming from both sides. Looking over the shoulder of one of his teammates, the Renegade looked down the barrel at a fast moving blur, and fired. The flare of muzzle flashes lit up his night vision in a random rhythm, clamped down from overwhelming his senses by the automatic filters on his glasses.

Loud cracks and pops surrounded him. There were already bodies piling up at both ends of the hallway. The creatures were fast and unnaturally strong, but they hadn't counted on the firepower or training of this group. Despite their disadvantages, technology and tactics won this battle for the Renegade.

And then as fast as it started it was over. The last shot echoed loudly, refusing to stop as it repeatedly found new bulkheads where it could reverberate.

The Renegade carefully approached the twisted mass of bodies before him and noticed that most of them were still moving. He began systematically stopping that movement, one head-shot at a time.

Chapter 40: The Ace and the Renegade

The Ace had known this was a bad idea from the beginning. It all felt wrong, like he had been unable to shake a constant early-morning hangover since the minute he transformed. Of course, he hadn't fed as often as the others. He was still too timid to get over the thought of hurting people to satiate himself, only giving in to hunger when it was at its most intense and he stopped having complete control over himself, the animal instinct temporarily overriding his conscious mind.

Now it was even worse. Staying on the repeater station, in charge of something. Placed above other people. He had done well with his career, but he was forever an individualist, never wanting to depend on others, or have them depend on him. This was all so new.

The Harbinger had left him behind after they had easily taken the repeater from the unarmed skeleton crew. He had thought the two of them had something...maybe still did. But obviously he valued it more than she did. After their fun and furiously fast time together he didn't want to be anywhere but near her. Now a vast expanse of emptiness separated them and he was feeling incredibly alone.

Then the gunfire started. It shook him up, but prompted no response. A fact that he observed about himself as if he were a spectral figment, watching his own life go by without any input or control. He was a deer staring into the bright shining headlights of some speeding hunk of metal, about to collide with his body while he stood mutely paralyzed, flight or fight response failing when it mattered most.

They had known someone would show up sooner or later. *The military?* But their ships were still on the radar, approaching fast, but not close enough to send a boarding party. Certainly the small shuttle detected earlier was a diplomatic mission, or refugees. They wouldn't assault on foot, would they? It seemed infinitely more likely to him that anyone who wanted to destroy this place would just blast the thing to smithereens. One well placed piece of ordinance ought to do it.

He stood alone in the command center, watching all the monitors, unable to think clearly, unwilling to commit to any course of action. Detached, he observed the team from the shuttle as they moved with practiced precision into the ambush and miraculously emerged victorious. Then another, smaller group appeared out of nowhere, materializing *behind* his defenders, and mopped up the rest of his scattered forces with ease.

He was the Ace in the hole. The trump card. The hard six. If anyone could get out of this situation, it was supposed to be him.

But he couldn't think. He was frozen, mind blank as freshly fallen snow.

He began to doubt the moniker. How desperate had she been to think that he could be a secret weapon? That he could win when the odds were low and the stakes were high?

He was trapped, an escape artist on stage, expected to perform a deadly routine without any training.

He didn't have the heart to go out fighting. If he fled they'd find him. Talking, discourse, *negotiation* was the only hope. He was simply a passive observer and he imagined whoever was heading this way would see that. Surely they would.

A knock on the door. He had forgotten that the command center had a little bit of extra security, though at the time the architects must have thought it foolish.

The thick door — an extravagant expense to bring up a gravity well — was locked with a heavy bolt. The Ace saw no reason to delay the inevitable. Either they'd find a way in here eventually or he'd starve to death.

With a firm thunk the bolt slid back. He opened the door, gesturing invitingly to those on the other side.

One soldier equipped with electronic sunglasses, light body armor, and a carbine strode through confidently to recon the room. He relaxed a bit after a cursory visual inspection. "Looks clear other than this guy," he said to someone outside, indicating the Ace with a shrug.

The next person to step through the threshold was eerily familiar. The Ace couldn't quite place him at first, but after a long, intense stare the connection clicked. He breathed a sigh of relief that this was someone he knew. Someone he could reason with.

The Renegade appeared to be going through the same process. His eyes narrowed to a squint and then recognition dawned on his face. He spoke first, their roles of interrogation reversed since their last encounter, "You…were you hiding in here? Were you their prisoner?"

The Ace half smiled at that. "I didn't want to be here, if that's what you're asking."

"This is the command center."

"Sure is! With all these monitors and readouts it has the best view of the whole place, inside and out."

The Renegade looked perturbed. He had noticed something about the Ace he didn't like. Or didn't trust. He was instantly edgy. "Can you open your mouth for me? Real wide?"

The Ace sighed. He had known the illusion wouldn't last. That he was a bit too awkward and not a good enough actor to keep up the charade for long. He had just hoped it would last more than a few seconds. He bared his teeth.

The Renegade snapped back, raising a sidearm the Ace hadn't noticed before. "You're one of them."

"Of course, why else would they put me in charge? You don't think they let just anyone into the command center, do you?"

"Then why didn't you attack us like your friends did? Were you in here to send a message back to the others?"

The Ace laughed. "No, that…that would've been a good idea. But I didn't even think of it. I froze. I don't want to hurt anyone. Never have. I don't have a violent bone in my body. It's turned into a real problem recently."

"I see, I think. So how are you transforming people?" The Renegade began pacing as he thought out loud. "The Doc must have left extensive documentation, because I assumed that his branch of the research died with him. That no new people were being changed. But given you and the others we've encountered here — the technology survived somehow. Did he leave a cache of supplies? Multiple injections could alter the body's entire DNA over time. Or maybe a pill? Though that would take even longer to administer."

"No no no. There's no extended process. No lab or equipment. No vials or syringes."

"Then how is this spreading? We've been around your kind and not contracted anything, so it can't be airborne or some kind of toxin. Unless... unless we're carriers now, waiting for symptoms to show after an incubation period."

"Wrong again. Look, I don't care if it's supposed to be a big secret. All the unInitiated probably have it figured out by now anyway, given the gossip. So here it is: it's a virus that carries new DNA and RNA to infect each new host. Multiplying itself as it changes the cells of the body it's in, waiting to be transmitted once more."

"I worked on this project and we never planned to use a virus as a transmission vector. There'd be no way to control it. No way to make sure that only those you wanted were transformed. No way to corner the market and maximize profits. That's why we relied on Cas9. But it wouldn't be impossible...a neutered version of HIV could work as a starting point for what you're describing. So what's the method of transmission?"

"Isn't it obvious? You pretty much arrived at it through your own deduction." The Ace waited, a patient teacher.

The Renegade's face became more creased, stern lines of muscles setting his jaw like a rusted hinge. "Sex. It spreads sexually."

He waited for the conclusion to smash into the Renegade. When it hit, it hit hard.

"An STD! The Doc used my work to make an STD!"

The Ace had forgotten all about the danger and death that had consumed the hallways outside a few minutes before and started using his hands as he talked, becoming more animated and feeling more alive than he had in weeks. *Finally, someone with half a brain to talk to.* "Bingo! So you see, it can be controlled, to some extent, on a case by case basis. The same way that genes have been spread — and selected — since life began. This next step in human evolution will be guided through the same channels it always has. Nature at its finest."

"And if the DNA of the hosts' cells changes, then there isn't a cure? You probably aren't even thinking about that side of things. We were originally working on a way to make sure the process was reversible, maybe even fast enough to be turned on at the beginning of a shift and then turned off when it's time to go home. But if what you're saying about the virus and infection is true...there'd be no original DNA in a host left for an antivirus to use in a reverse transformation."

"Sure. It acts like most uncured STDs that way. Once you have it, you have it, and without protection you're going to give it to whoever you sleep with."

The Renegade considered that for a long moment. His face growing darker and more furrowed. "And the communication with the others: it's a tight beam laser or maser, directional, so that it doesn't release EM waves into space and thus can't be tracked from anywhere but this station?"

The Ace was confused. This was a sudden turn from talking about the transformation that had left him with more strength and abilities and keen senses than he had ever imagined and was so excited to share. "Well, yeah, we have an antenna dish that is auto-tracking a set location. It's partially why I'm here: if a micro-meteorite dislodges it or knocks it out of alignment we have to repair it ASAP. There are some spares down in the—"

The Renegade interrupted him. "That's all I needed to know."

"No, stop!" The Ace raised his hands to cover his face while looking away in fright and protest but the Renegade just shot through his palms, three rounds thrumming with energy as they spun out of the pistol's barrel, spinning and ripping the soft tissue apart before crashing through the Ace's skull with sickening wet crunches, bursting out the other side to finish their journeys by thudding into the wall.

"Get me the coordinates that dish is locked onto," the Renegade said to no one in particular as he walked away from the bloody mess.

"Sir, wait!" One of his soldiers pleaded.

He turned back, impatient.

"Look! On the monitors!"

He saw it then. Four ships inbound.

They hadn't searched the whole repeater. There might be Infected they hadn't found. Valuable intel. Life-saving supplies.

Resigned, he admitted to himself that none of that mattered now.

They were out of time.

"The coordinates. Don't worry about anything else. Get them and run!" The Renegade ordered.

He took his own advice and started sprinting back to the shuttle, thinking to himself: *Force is all-conquering, but its victories are short-lived.*

Chapter 41: The Captain

The loud crack of the gunshot into the Lawyer's face jolted everyone else from a trance. Her head snapped back unnaturally from the force of the extra-large caliber round, something unusual the Captain had brought along given the unknown abilities of these strange new creatures. Now, as he was sprayed with blood and gore, he was extremely thankful for that foresight.

The other pale traitors echoed their fallen icon and pounced toward the marines, who had been smart enough to keep their distance after initially herding the others away from the console. Automatic rifle fire burst loudly through the confined air, sending shockwaves out in a wake, sure to get the rest of the sleeping crew out of their beds.

The mutiny was finished. The Captain's adrenaline was still spiking though, and he knew from experience that there was more to come.

He turned back to the console to check the communication logs, a hunch based on the fact that the Lawyer was preparing for the possibility that she might not have to fire on all the other ships. They were getting dangerously close to the repeater and he knew this confrontation would be over by the time they reached it.

The logs didn't give anything away at first glance. No blatant treachery. But there might be clues and patterns embedded in the signals. He'd need time to investigate. Time he didn't have.

There *was* a recent entry recording a failed attempt to hail a shuttle leaving the repeater. It scurried away like a starving rat with a newfound crumb. Perhaps, after securing the repeater itself, that shuttle would be their next prey.

The hunt was on.

The lines were drawn.

The ram had touched the wall.

He felt a surge of excitement now that the first blood was spilled. Here in the stars he felt closer to those old gods that the ancients looked up to in the heavens. A god of war might seem like a quaint romantic notion, outdated and barbaric, but he knew the truth of things: war was inevitable, and anything with that relentless, unstopping certainty deserved to be worshiped. The sun, the moon, war and famine, he knew these were constants, dependable as gravity and thermodynamics. Unconsciously he scanned for that dusty red body which bore Ares' Latin name — his patron for this day of grim duty — and this close to the inside of the asteroid belt it was also the nearest planet.

Just as these unbidden thoughts took hold of his mind the ship lurched. One of the marines shouted as it pitched and rumbled, hit by some exterior force. The Captain switched the console from his investigation of the communication logs to a real-time tactical interface.

That rocking had been high energy laser or maser fire coming from one of the other ships. One of *his* ships! *Superstition be damned,* he thought. Some trickster god like Loki must be the one looking over his shoulder today.

The tactical readout was fully updated and tracking all the other ships and their respective statuses now. The *Murad* was still showing all systems normal, it was the farthest out and would be the first to reach the repeater. *Which may or may not be a good thing,* he reminded himself.

The *Qianlong* had stopped responding to automatic pings and appeared dead in the water. External scans showed only sporadic electromagnetic activity but even more worrying was that the ship had vented all pressure, which shouldn't have been possible. Even in non-emergency mode there were bulkheads to prevent a cataclysmic depressurization from wiping out the whole ship. So it hadn't been an accident. *Sabotage.* Unless they had foreknowledge and been in suits everyone on board was dead. *The poor sobs.*

And most distressing of all was the *Cromwell,* which had used maneuvering thrusters to pull off a momentum-conserving flip, showing him its face and firing on him with its forward banks.

Another burst rocked the *Jackson* and the Captain held himself steady, bracing his hands on either side of the console. The readouts indicated that they were being hit by impulse beams of ultraviolet light. The hard radiation packed the most punch of any non-explosive armament these ships carried. The diamond-mirror outer carapace was shielding them from the worst of it by reflecting most of the energy away, shining faces scattering it into harmless rainbows, but the effect was not fully negating all the propelled energy, the remnants of which ate into the absorptive lead hull, causing the ship to buck at odd angles.

If the *Cromwell* had been firing missiles the Captain suspected the *Jackson* would be disabled already, possibly destroyed. A surprise attack from their own ships had not been something the design committee had considered, and it would have been devastating if properly executed. Luckily his nameless foes — he suspected they were last-minute additions to their crews like the Lawyer had been — either didn't know how to configure the tracking system, didn't have the arming codes, or were purposefully trying to conserve the limited munitions the ship came with. He considered that each possibility was more likely than the previous, and the last one frightened him immensely. It bespoke considerable foresight; a deep understanding of the macro and micro situations paired with tactics he hadn't anticipated. It was the exact combination of traits he had hoped never to encounter in a real enemy. *The planning involved! They must've had someone on the inside since the beginning.* He had thought them isolated on the fringes of human space, but clearly they had infiltrated his ranks. It was a depressing revelation that he was at a disadvantage before the battle even began. He resolved that it wouldn't happen again.

Warning signals flashed amber, indicating that the heat exchangers would not be able to handle the constant, concentrated barrage of energy at the fore. They needed time to cool down, but the capacitors charging the ultraviolet rays on the *Cromwell* were regular like clockwork. He had already lost, simply by not firing first.

Another blast rocked the *Jackson,* nearly throwing the Captain off his feet. The incredibly expensive, inches-thick shielding was almost gone at some points, melting from its precise crystal matrix into useless slag.

He thought furiously, running through options and alternatives faster than he ever had before: he had to survive, to explain what had happened on his ship and to the others, and he couldn't get out a message that clearly recounted events fast enough if he stayed here. He couldn't win this fight.

Resolved, he armed every missile the *Jackson* had, and fired.

Half of the missiles rushed to the nearby *Cromwell,* which immediately switched targeting solutions to send the high-frequency beams at the incoming threats. The missiles juked and danced, their automated systems trying to fly in unpredictable, random paths to avoid being destroyed before intercepting their target. The *Cromwell's* computers did their job as well as could be expected given the short distance involved, allowing only a single lone missile to slip by. It detonated right on their nose, and the ship stopped firing, at least temporarily. The Captain switched to a camera view and could see atmosphere venting from a hull breach. The ship was damaged, but salvageable.

The other half of the missiles had longer flight paths, heading straight for the repeater, which was still several minutes out.

The Captain flipped the *Jackson* around and throttled up the main engines to build up delta velocity compared to the other ships.

Everything shrank until finally he couldn't see anything from the camera, so he switched back to an icon sensor view. The missiles were still on their way, the *Cromwell* unable to intercept them.

The *Qianlong* was still unmoving. A massive metal fossil, petrified, hanging silently in space.

But the *Murad,* which previously hadn't moved from its course to the repeater, started a sluggish arcing turn. It was still ahead of the missiles, and its main banks didn't have line of sight on them from this angle...*Oh no.*

He watched in excruciatingly slow motion as the trillion dollar investment aligned itself to block the path from the missiles to the repeater.

Their targeting systems tried to compensate, but given their speed the ship's broadside was simply too big a target to miss.

A dozen impact points. Each a tiny blip on his screen, but representing thousands of tons of force, chemical compounds turned into raw kinetic energy in the blink of an eye.

For a moment he thought the *Murad* had succeeded. That the sacrifice had made his mission of disabling or destroying the repeater a failure. But then an unfamiliar warning signal flared deep carmine on his screen.

Unable to maintain containment, the *Murad's* fusion core was undergoing a wild, uncontrolled escalation.

The Captain did the only thing he could: as quickly as possible he entered the sequence of commands to disable all the electronics on the ship. He knew he was still within range of the electromagnetic pulse that the ship-turned-nuclear-bomb would generate, and if it hit the *Jackson* in its current state and fried all the necessary components to keep the ship running...he just hoped he was fast enough.

In an instant all the interior light died. An unpowered fiber optic cable gave him a single tiny window to the outside, revealing microscopic stars spattered in ink. A breath later and a bright, unnaturally white light erupted, briefly illuminating the bridge, the effect similar to lightning piercing clouds in a midnight storm. The *Murad* was gone.

Given its proximity to the repeater, the detonation had suddenly turned this mission into an unexpected Pyrrhic success.

But the cost... The only one who triumphed today was the god of war.

The Captain slumped against the console and started waiting until it was safe to turn the lights back on.

Chapter 42: The Harbinger and the Minion

She left him there.

At the time it seemed like the best course of action. To prove to him — and to herself — that she didn't need him. That this was on her terms. Under her control. Merely convenient.

So she left him there.

It was a failed experiment from the start. One that she had planned on rectifying as soon as possible. It had proven the exact opposite of what she wanted it to. She felt that perhaps this was a remnant of her humanity, something she wished could be excised, through surgery or gene therapy: she could control a vast multitude of people, technology, and resources, but she couldn't control her own heart. She could no more will it to stop feeling than she could to stop beating. And she had tried. Desperately.

She now oscillated between lashing out at herself for being so careless with the one life that mattered and replaying the myriad decisions that led her to this place. There were stupendously large, deliberate choices — transforming him, leaving him on that doomed repeater — and infinitesimally tiny moments she never would've recalled without this tragedy magnifying them. A kiss on her shoulder. The way his hair looked when he first woke up. Even the peaceful, almost innocent face he made while sleeping.

And then the guilt came rushing in. Guilt not just at what she had done, but guilt at a new emotion, one easily identified, amalgamated though it was with all the others: relief. Relief at his passing, at his knowledge and experiences dissipating into the abyss forever. He had known her true name. She was no longer vulnerable to *kotodama* from him. The relief was a betrayal. A sign that she never fully trusted him. Proof that her own shortcomings were the ultimate cause of his demise.

Guilt piled on guilt, smothering words floating across her vision like *honor* and *duty* and *sacrifice*. Guilt pierced those concepts with a spear, their lifeblood dripping out, clear and runny, exposing them for what they were: excuses.

For the moment, she pushed all of that down, trying to force it out of her conscious mind. Her efforts succeeded, to an extent. She dried her eyes and attempted a smile, found she couldn't. A stern, angry face was easier — a shield that would hold for longer.

The Minion entered her asteroid offices. His body was still mending itself from the multiple explosions suffered, some limited form of eyesight most recently returned. It was painfully unfair that the universe had kept this nuisance alive while her Ace had been obliterated.

She had been working on something here when the news came in, and wanted to summon it back to the forefront of her mind so she had something to talk about, but found she had no memory of whatever it was. All the events happening across the entire universe seemed unimportant in this moment.

The Minion eventually grew impatient, or possibly just uncomfortable with her silence, and skipped straight to business: "You know that because the repeater has been destroyed we're out of communication with Earth again. The good news is the final combat analysis finished and none of the scans show any of the warships ever docking with the repeater. So we can assume our position here is still unknown, since they would've had to manually inspect the line-of-sight array to find us." He paused for a moment, but she offered no comment. "You've reviewed the proposals? Do you have orders for how to proceed?"

She recalled what she had decided straightaway and took one final gulp before trusting herself to talk. Her voice remained thankfully unbroken. "Yes, let's tow one of the raided stations into the relay's place. Whichever is nearest." It was an inspired, scrappy idea she was proud of.

She could see the skepticism twist the Minion's face. "That may take some time. And a lot of people."

"Yes," she said flatly to his unasked question. *It is worth it to stay here and use an intermediary link.* If they had all been living on a single station with open communication...

"And there's no guarantee we'll be able to keep this one up and running either," he continued. "Earth will be watching."

"There's no guarantee for anything in life. We're all lost, wandering in the woods alone. We must simply keep putting one foot in front of the other, looking for a way out." She took a breath to steady herself. "And learn from our mistakes. This time we'll have ships at our disposal. A flare gun, carried into the woods. Any word on repairs?"

"The *Qianlong* is ready to go."

"Good, then have it escort a shuttle on the towing operation. And the other?"

"The *Cromwell's* repairs are still underway. Even given its capabilities and extreme engineering they pushed it to the max in its fight with the *Jackson.* Finding enough high quality diamond to replace the outer hull is proving...difficult. We suspect they mass produced it in a lab, but we don't have that kind equipment."

"Have everyone that is not engaged with setting up the new repeater or our habitat here working on it. The diamond the asteroid field yields will have to suffice."

"We don't have a lot of technical expertise to go around, and training others for repairs and mining would add a huge upfront lag time—"

She held up a hand to prevent him from prattling on. "Pull whoever you need from the habitat building operations then. Having that ship in full working order is the priority."

"Fine. Anything else?"

She glared, shooing him out in dismissal.

As the Minion walked away she realized she was entrusting a lot to him. To everyone she was working with here. It was a novel sensation for her, consciously giving up control.

But if recent events had taught her anything, it was that keeping too much invested in a single person led to devastating results when that person was gone. *Even when it's the closest person to you.*

Even if you leave him.

Chapter 43: The Major General and the Captain

The Major General had shuttled up to the shipyards to once more meet the Captain in person. This was very unlike him, and showed just how angry and concerned he was. The Captain was having a hard time guessing which emotion dominated.

When he entered the small makeshift office the Major General stood up and approached him, looking like he was about to go on an exasperating tirade. But then he closed his mouth right after he opened it. Instead, he sighed and started again. "The first line of defense was the battleships. They could go anywhere within a decent range of Earth, so we could send them to proactively hunt down anyone left alive with this infection. Now…well as soon as word of the outcome of the battle reached us we started building more ships. We've been busy during your time in transit. It's not like we dismantled the shipyards as soon as the first fleet was finished. We just didn't expect to need more than we had, and the cost of each one is enormous: a significant percentage of the global GDP. We're going to have to start borrowing against our collective future. But now that the enemy has a ship or two of their own I don't think convincing the decision-makers will be much of a problem. I had originally hoped the *Qianlong* would be salvageable if we mounted a recovery op, but the scans showed it moving away shortly after you left the area. They must've gotten to it right away. Which speaks volumes. We can only hope they're still on the defensive, recovering, waiting. Because if they strike now, two ships against one…

"The question is, Captain, what the hell happened out there?"

The Captain realized this wouldn't be the dressing down and immediate court marshal he had been expecting. At least not yet. Slightly relieved, he tried to explain: "It was the hardest kind of sabotage to overcome, sir: social engineering. I'm certain they had agents on each of the ships, who clearly managed a successful mutiny on the *Cromwell*, depressurized the *Qianlong*, and changed the trajectory of the *Murad* at the last second. We may never know exactly what happened on each of them, but it almost happened to us as well. You saw my preliminary report. It was a near thing even on the *Jackson*."

The Major General nodded. "That's why you're still in command, Captain. Yours was the only ship unscathed. You've proven you're trustworthy *and* capable of quickly responding to dire situations, whereas everyone else failed us on at least one of those two counts. Have you had time to think about a better filter for the next round of recruits?"

"I'd like to personally interview every new candidate. I know what to look for."

"That will leave you very little time for anything else. But even if you could teach others I don't think I could implicitly trust anyone else with the job. There's no choice then. Proceed with the interviews."

"Aye, sir. There's also a matter of the corpses we accrued during the action. Analyzing them might reveal some weaknesses we can exploit."

"Of course, those macabre details. We have a facility ground-side that's already dedicated. I'll see they're shipped down ASAP."

"Thank you, sir. Was there anything else?"

"Yes, unfortunately. First, we finally have a name for this threat. Someone returned to the origin station and used our comm network. We decoded the traffic, and found messages referring to the genetically modified as the Infected. It's informal, but it'll do for now.

"Second, I'd like your input on our last line of defense. It seems you won't be sleeping very much in the coming weeks. We're building unmanned artillery satellites: orbital defense platforms. We'll have enough to create a very thin net covering the Earth. There won't be any gaps unless one gets knocked out. So if for some reason the next wave of battleships fails to intercept a transport they are plan B. We have to prevent the Infected from reaching the surface at all costs. They could come down anywhere: completely off the grid in a remote jungle, at a rendezvous with a ship in the middle of the ocean, or in a big enough park inside a metropolis. So if they're even remotely capable of thinking ahead we won't be able to stop them before they spread. We won't be able to find them in time."

"Sir, do we know anything else about their motivations? Certainly the people over in intelligence must have some theories. And the Infected must know they're carrying a disease at this point, how could they be so careless spreading it around? It's inhuman."

"You're still thinking like a soldier, willing to sacrifice himself for the greater good. But it's very human to want to survive and live comfortably. It's simple selfishness. They're trapped in space, we've quarantined them forever, so they'll start thinking of a future without ever setting foot on Earth again. Any forced exile or imprisonment is bearable if there's belief that it's temporary. Humans can keep hope alive even when it should be long dead. *If* there's a chance of escape, of appeal. But if you know for certain that you'll be stuck in one tiny space station for the rest of your life, never meeting anyone new, never going back to your favorite restaurant, never having any of your vices available, then hope and reason go out the airlock. They'll be desperate to get back on the ground. To the point of putting their own lives at risk. And if you're willing to sacrifice your own life to achieve your goals, then what of the lives of others?"

"That makes sense, although it's horribly selfish. If the disease can't be cured, then no amount of quarantine or waiting for it to die out will make them less of a threat. They must realize that. And if it's fatal they could kill millions. Maybe billions if it's not stopped."

"Precisely. That could be the second reason, selfishness aside."

The Captain was clearly shocked. "What? You think they'd commit genocide on purpose?"

"There are those — and I mean members of top secret think tanks — that have postulated that a cataclysmic disease is the perfect solution to most of Earth's problems. The rates of hunger and poverty, the price of food, water, and oil, they're going to keep increasing. Nothing reasonable we do on this planet will prevent that by the time we start running out. And it's all due to population.

"The best way, in *my* opinion, to solve all our impending problems would be to start colonizing other planets. That's what some of the research on our now defunct stations was working toward. Mars would be ideal, obviously, with its limited geological activity. There are no cryovolcanoes or methane storms. It's reasonably hospitable to human life — aside from the cold and lack of an atmosphere — and especially when compared to a lot of the other nearby options. We couldn't very well survive inside a gas giant. Some of their moons, sure, but on the other side of the asteroid belt they're just that much farther away. Away from the sun's life-giving light. Away from the Earth as a fall back and resupply. As an alternative, the asteroids themselves might be a good bet. Some of them are very resource rich.

"But that's still science fiction at this point. We've been dreaming of colonization for too long without actually doing it. Now it's too little too late.

"So what's left? An Earth consumed by civil war. Where it's going to spark first, whether it's over a potato or the last piece of copper wire, we have no way of predicting. For some, the very wealthiest, they may not feel physically threatened by such an idea because they can afford security, home defenses, second homes and private yachts to fall back to in the worst-case scenarios. But their profits are threatened. They need reliable infrastructure to support shipping goods to consumers. Electricity and networks for information services. Even if those things disappeared *temporarily* they might be able to rebuild without irreparable losses. But if the conflict lasted any length of time very few would be able to emerge on the other side intact.

"I've had to think about this a lot because I interact with these people. A few steps up the ladder and they're my bosses. They're everyone's bosses.

"Now imagine that you own a piece of land. It houses a huge office complex, full of buildings and data and personnel. How do you really own that land? Legally, it's a piece of paper with a name on it filed in a county office somewhere. If a civil war breaks out and that land gets occupied by rebels, or bombed by the government, then what do you have? Nothing. If you can't protect your land then you never really own it. That's part of the reason the Company has started to invest more in private security. They see the end to this stability coming. But men on the ground with guns in their hands can only get you so far. Human bodies can't stop bombs dropped by drones at thirty thousand feet.

"Even if this hypothetical conflict ends, who knows what you'll be coming back to. There are stories of the end of World War II, of Jewish refugees returning from the torture of concentration camps to their fully paid for, legally owned homes in Germany or Poland. And they get there, having survived the whole war, with nothing left except this little plot of land they remember from a different, better life, only to be murdered by their neighbors who never left. Because they wanted a bigger house. Or to have more room for farming. To own a factory. A storefront. In the time between when the cease fire is called and life returns to normal, killing a family for their land could easily be gotten away with. Just blame it on the Nazis. No one would blink twice. No one would call the police and demand an investigation. There would be no manhunt, no fear of repercussion. A convenient, believable scapegoat makes it much easier to get away with heinous crimes, or even consider committing them in the first place. The fact that a piece of paper with a name on it might have still existed somewhere meant nothing during that post-war chaos.

"What I'm getting at is that the wealthiest, most influential people in society depend on at least some level of stability. Sure, the occasional, *isolated* conflict might be good for their profits — depending on what they do — but they need to trust in the system of laws within the countries they primarily reside in. If that comes into question, if they start thinking that the yellowed, brittle piece of paper in that manila folder inside the olive-colored stainless steel cabinet in the damp basement of the county filing office might no longer *mean* anything, then their whole way of life is at risk. Their status at the top of the food chain comes into doubt. And they are going to do anything within their considerable power to stop that from happening.

"That's where disease comes in. Because the fundamental problem is population. Simply the raw numbers of us. There are too many humans to feasibly sustain what we do to this planet every day. And we keep popping out more at an exponential rate. But you can't just start killing people. Inevitably you get caught or someone's relative or lover wants to take revenge. No matter *how* you choose who to kill, it will be a wrong choice. No criteria will ever work. You will never be forgiven. So you need something random. Indiscriminate. With no way of tracing back to you. There are some diseases that might target a specific race or people with certain traits. But a lot of them don't care. They'll kill any human as likely as the next. The rich are in the best position to survive it, because they can afford to be away from any exceptionally bad disease centers. Private jets and helicopters provide a quick escape from anywhere. Even if they did get sick, they're also able to pay for the best healthcare, and therefore have a higher chance to survive even if they do contract it. And when it's over, who do you blame? If it was random, untargeted, and it doesn't seem like it was caused by anyone, then you're left with a tragedy. No one to come take revenge. No one to hunt you down. And assuming that we haven't been completely wiped out as a species, that the fatality rate isn't 100% — and it never is, no disease in history has ever been completely fatal, someone always survives thanks to evolution and our amazing physiological ability to adapt — then at the end we as a society have a bit more breathing room. Time to become more efficient. Go green. Launch those colony ships. The influenza epidemic of 1919 is a perfect example of this. Or the bubonic plague in the middle ages. They took out whole percentage points of the world's population. If that hadn't happened, if all of those millions of people who died had survived and had children, and their children had children, and so on, where would we be today? Would we have had the resources to even get this far? Or would we have begun fighting and killing each other over vegetables, grains, and fresh water a century ago?

"I don't agree with causing innocent people to suffer to solve our problems. I think we have a duty to stop anyone who does. But you have to admit the idea has merit. And that is the very worst kind of idea."

Chapter 44: The Lion

She let her hair flow free during her sessions in the Dungeon. It was the last remnant of her former life finally allowed to be itself. She had always maintained proper grooming before. Brushing it every night. Putting it up or in a pony tail whenever she was in public. Only ever letting it down in quiet moments by herself.

Now her wild mane was an untamable, tangled mess, a thing of legend among the gossip she knew happened when those in her Enclave swapped stories about their experiences in the Dungeon. It was something she loosely encouraged, bringing them closer together and inciting some friendly competition.

Inevitably, it was during one of the pleasantly exhausting peaks of one of those sessions when she got word the scouts had seen something. The fact that she had been interrupted here in her sacred sanctum spoke to how serious the threat was. They had an entire electronic alerting suite set up, powered by the solar panels and their newly installed batteries, including motion sensors and real-time camera feeds sent to computer vision systems. But she had insisted on real people scouting the surrounding area, as well as lookouts on the roof both day and night. There were some things humans were still better at than computers, faster when seconds were critical and time translated into lives. Such as recognizing threats.

The police were coming.

So the Lion cut her session short, freeing her partner and instructing him to get ready as she was about to do, when she would have preferred to leave him chained up against the wall, forced to wait, squirming in anticipation of the conclusion yet to come.

This moment had been inevitable ever since she had finally discovered the secret weapon that the Veteran had used to gather the

Initiates in the first place. The true power behind any exclusive club or religion: not money or sex appeal, but fear. And not fear of just anything. Fear of *loss*. It drove the subconscious of so many people, animal brains blindly concerned with survival, which so often depended on protecting and preserving what one had, with avoiding pain, so that the emotional force behind fearing loss acted like a wrecking ball when its full weight bore down.

After this epiphany the Lion was able to adapt the Enclave's marketing and recruiting tactics to appeal to a much wider base. For many it spoke to the loss of their friends or family or lovers, promising that it would never happen again thanks to longevity and health. For the poor, who, having the fewest possessions, were the the most materialistic, it meant giving them strength to protect what they owned. The only people she couldn't reach with this message were those who had never wanted for anything, never experienced true loss. And those were few people indeed.

The Enclave saw explosive growth.

Now they were paying for it.

As she moved into her bedroom and changed into clothes a bit less conspicuous, she was confident she knew how to respond to the police. Others had already come from the power company. They were tradesmen in overalls, bored with their jobs, their lives, despite all the amazing things happening to humanity around the globe every day. She was part of a hidden world, enticing because it was foreign and secret. Combined with a healthy dose of fear-mongering based on her earlier revelation, most had acceded quickly when she put this strange new life lacking loss within their grasp. Those unwilling she simply took by force. They needed a growing stock of food source anyway.

The police needed to be handled differently. They were coming to investigate the previous disappearances here, and would probably suspect the cause, correctly. They'd be loaded for bear.

She became the Mouse again, at least in outward appearance. Her internal demeanor was unaffected by the clothes she wore or putting her hair back into its simple pony tail. She was not the loose, dull sweater she wore. Nor the ripped, baggy jeans. For once in her life she knew exactly who she was, what she wanted, and that her looks were a means to an end, not a static, defining characteristic.

She gave orders and words of assurance to everyone she passed — they had drilled this before but never put it to the test until now. For the most part they moved confidently into position. Regardless of what happened tonight she was proud of them. Proud of herself for creating something here, not only the physical aspects, but a community of people that trusted each other, trusted *her* with their lives. She moved everyone that needed to breathe into the basement bomb shelter, and told all the Initiates to hide in their preassigned ambush positions along the hallways.

She opened the main door and stepped out into a chill, twilight evening. The sunlight hit the atmosphere and the buildings at the perfect angle to reflect in golden hues, washing the open landscape before her in a magical aura. It was as if the universe conspired in this timing, speaking to her and saying, *Anything can happen, anything is possible.*

Knowing this would be a no-knock raid, she opted to leave the door open to avoid damage if they tried to break it down. The Lion put on her best demure mask, took a deep breath, and started running toward the flashing lights.

She could see now that a SWAT van accompanied the normal white-striped sedans. She put her hands up while shouting, "Help! Don't shoot! I need help!"

The vehicles twisted into breaking turns, showing her their broadsides, throwing up dirt and coming to a halt less than a hundred yards from the building. After cutting the sirens and filing out one of the officers yelled at her, "Stop right there! No further!"

"Ok, ok!" she stopped running. "I'll do anything, please! We need to get inside! I found people, they're hurt. *Bleeding.*" She said it like she'd never seen blood before.

There was some hesitation. This was probably their worst fear. But if they could do something to help, to save those meaningless, unfulfilled lives inside…she was banking on their humanity and the urgency that any first responder knew from experience would mean the difference between life and death for a victim.

She heard some muted conferring, maybe a radio call, then, "Fine, we're going in, but you're staying out here."

She slumped at that internally, but outwardly nodded. It was an eventuality they had considered, even if it was less than ideal. She couldn't lead them into the exact position for maximum carnage inside, but previous work had manipulated the interior environment to naturally guide the cops down the optimal path.

They moved her near a squad car to wait with two of the officers who would stay outside with the vehicles. "Where are they?" one them asked.

"Just up the stairs, on the second floor." That would make sure they didn't try to get into the basement bomb shelter first, where some people were being kept against their will and hoping beyond hope for this very rescue that was now occurring above their heads.

The SWAT team moved off at a jogging pace. They were well-armored, but their equipment was meant for defending against firearms. Close quarters meant trading rifles for shotguns, while still wearing the same bullet proof vests and helmets.

Yet the natural instinct of the creatures they were fighting was to go for the neck. Men's formal clothing revolved around collars, a fashion statement originally meant to invoke the image of a knight and the associated neck protection provided by steel armor. Medieval people knew that the neck was one of the most vulnerable places on the body. And, despite the hints in modern clothing and the available histories of warfare, these *professionals* went into battle utterly unprepared. Wrapped up in their reality of guns and technology, they had forgotten even the basics learned by people killing people throughout earlier centuries.

On top of her disgust rose a wave of excitement she hadn't been expecting. This is what they planned for. Trained for over-and-agonizing-time-over again. Now all that preparation came down to a single, tense moment where anything could happen.

There were short, sporadic bursts of gunfire. The sound echoed throughout the building before escaping and washing over the three of them standing outside.

She knew what was happening inside right now. The Initiates had hidden themselves in the shadows and cubicles and doorways and waited for the SWAT team to move in. They had patiently stayed silent — not even breathing — and when the last cop was through the door they pounced simultaneously.

The fight would be brief and fierce. SWAT was trained to aim for center of mass. It was the biggest target and the most likely to stop an enemy combatant. A chestful or gutful of buckshot would certainly disable one of her people, but it wouldn't kill them outright. And they had two distinct and crucial advantages: numbers and surprise. Leaping out of the darkness with their ghost skin and razor teeth must have made them look like nightmares come to life. She wistfully wished she had seen them in action.

The clap of the last shot died out. The ambush was over. She swore she could feel a sense of triumphant satisfaction emanating from the now eerily serene building.

Lost in her imaginings the Lion hadn't noticed the frantic reactions of the two remaining cops beside her.

"I can't raise anybody!" one of them yelled, far too loud given his partner's proximity.

"We should get in there," the other responded.

"No, we need to call for backup. We don't know what happened."

"They could be bleeding out right now!"

While they argued with each other she mused on how they hadn't even bothered to pat down this helpless girl who was now behind them and a few feet away. They paid her no attention while the debate got increasingly more heated, both staring intently at the building, willing x-ray vision upon themselves to see through the brick and concrete to determine the state of their fellow officers.

She pulled out the .40 caliber subcompact pistol she had hidden in the folds of her outfit and shot them both in the back. Twice. For good measure.

It was *some* justice for the Princess. But not all there was. There would be more to come.

There would *always* be more.

Chapter 45: The Renegade

The waves were thunder in his ears. They pounded into him, splashing off in every direction. Incessant.

He could feel the exfoliating affect on his skin. The tension seeping from every muscle. The power behind them exhausted.

He felt that he wasn't sad. More that a sadness was upon him. Language trapped his thinking. Left his thoughts without the ability to convey the weight of this external force concisely. Nonetheless, the emotion was something external. He could not control it.

The Renegade turned the knob clockwise hard and fast. The water slowed to a drip, and after a long moment of trying to push out one more drop, stopped.

He resolved that he would go to a real ocean whenever he got back to Earth. It would be the first thing he did. Somewhere beautiful and warm with that rhythmic crashing sound. He hadn't heard it in years, instead being trapped by the forever buzz of lights and electronics, inescapable on stations and shuttles.

The Renegade watched the water fall off himself, each drop splattering on the floor, and marveled at his own luck. He'd gambled in a game that risked death but paid out only knowledge: the location of the Infected base. And he'd beaten the house.

We're going to assault an asteroid. It was a heady thought for his animal brain to comprehend. Almost like it was happening to someone else. Like this wasn't his life anymore.

He knew on some level that long-term fatigue was setting in. Physical, mental, it didn't matter. He *needed* to be somewhere remote. Away from everything.

Of course, he realized, he was already as far from anywhere on Earth as he could be. But that wasn't the point of a vacation. Despite being in outer space with only a couple hundred humans within a million miles this is where his life was. His work. His love. And for a few short days he wanted to forget all about it. Removing himself physically seemed the only way.

But that was later, when he had finished wiping the Infected from the universe.

You can't go on vacation until your work is done.

Chapter 46: The Harbinger

The Harbinger was making a simple todo list while sipping tea in the very first cafe up and running in the asteroid habitat. It was a cramped room with curving walls the same dull gunk-brown color as the rest of the rock, a fact which the proprietor was trying to disguise with rectangular tapestries and prints, as well as a generous amount of organic matter — vines and flowers hung in about a quarter of the area, and would rapidly overtake it all if they had their way. She was grateful for the green. It had been uncommon in the necessary-for-science sterility of the old stations. It made the air here taste better. Fresh. She made a note on her pad to allocate more hydroponics room for replicating aesthetic plants.

Once the Harbinger realized Earth had thrown everything it had at them, there was a crucial decision to make: did she immediately counter-attack? A swift and righteous retribution was tempting. *So tempting.* They had two ships, Earth had one. And the Ace's murder screamed for justice in her mind. At first glance it seemed they could eliminate the only threat to their continued survival and gain dominance on top of the gravity well in one fell swoop. Some of her people — the Minion chief among them — had clamored for this option. It had a high chance of success. But it was also a gamble. What other defenses did Earth have in near-orbit? Were there surface-to-space ballistic missiles that had enough range to enter the fight? Cold War era satellite batteries with nukes still waiting for a target? There were too many unknowns. Losing both ships in a failed action against almighty Earth was far too big a risk. It would spell the ultimate end for her budding colony.

The safer course was defense. Wait for the enemy to expose itself and make the first move. So she restrained herself, restrained her people, the reins of her will around the popular opinion stretching until they almost snapped. Yet they held. Would hold. For a time.

Initially she thought of the ships merely as shields. And they could certainly provide protection. But in gaining control of two of the four sent to defeat her she had unknowingly committed the greatest heist in all of human history. She was an accidental pirate.

Proud of her acquisition, she learned all she could about the vessels. And upon hearing their original names she had been disgusted. They had perversely been paying homage to the worst murderers and maddest rulers from each country. She knew that to most Americans — probably including those who had been serving aboard it — *Jackson* was just a name on ancient paper money. The true histories had been scrubbed clean: every digital reference to the atrocities committed by any American official found and replaced by a more palatable story. To get to the truth, one had to find and read a physical book from ages past, most likely a large textbook or encyclopedia. But they were rare treasures nowadays, most hidden away in secret stashes, under the constant threat of fire, moths, or discovery. Luckily for her, training in the covert Japanese forces, while eschewing the ancient wisdom of *know thyself,* held on to the equally old and valuable adage *know thy enemy.*

So the Harbinger continued the pirate practice of renaming seized ships, while still keeping the country of origin intact. Thus the *Cromwell* and the *Qianlong* became the *Edward Teach* and the *Ching Shih.* It was a minor, symbolic thing, but she felt in her soul that it *mattered.*

In addition to the renaming she had her software people scrub as much as they could from the ships' operating systems and firmware, replacing everything with well-understood and publicly-researched open source code. She did not trust that there wasn't some sort of backdoor access implanted in the ships, and she didn't want to find that she was suddenly locked out at a crucial moment.

Once they had total control of the ships, including unlimited access to the diagnostic schematics, she had begun to realize the full cost of building a warship in space. It was, in a word, astronomical. The blueprints alone were worth enough to buy multiple countries outright. The total cost of the upfront research and development plus the construction and its required resources — both human and material — put a dent in the entire global economic output.

Knowing all that begged multiple questions. Given enough time and the right people, the Harbinger could replicate what they had done and build more ships of her own. Although the engineering was precise there wasn't any revolutionary science behind it that prevented it from being copied. The asteroid belt held a plethora of elements from when the solar system first formed, easily mined, so that side of things was solvable. But where could she get people with the required skills to construct it? The ones up here were a hodgepodge collection of survivors, not a full ecosystem of human potential. Their areas of expertise didn't cover everything she needed, not by a long shot.

Even if her propaganda programs could solve that problem eventually, she admitted to herself that the other issue couldn't be solved: did she have enough time?

No.

Fortunately, it might not matter. If she hunkered down and waited, Earth would inevitably build more ships for her. It was the only move they could make. They had to answer this threat. But they would be more prepared this time. More cautious about social hacking and who they let anywhere near the new ships. She thanked the ghost of the Doc profusely for his contingency plan that got Initiates off the original station and into position quickly enough to stage successful mutinies on three of the four ships. She hadn't been in close communication with them — it was a necessary precaution on the infiltrators' parts — so she didn't know all the details she needed to.

Where are the shipyards? It was the most pressing question for which she didn't have an answer. None of the Doc's agents had been able to record the precise location while they were on board. She couldn't fault them for being overly focused on their own missions, considering the outcome. When they examined the ships' logs and backtraced the vectors they found nothing in that region of space. Were the shipyards in an irregular orbit or somewhere off the path they hadn't looked yet? Had they been moved after the assault? Could the logs have been scrubbed as a final security precaution when the ships were launched? Were the shipyards stealthed in an unknown way? There were no clues. She was stuck.

The Harbinger found herself unconsciously tapping her finger on the pad, nervousness escaping physically. If she could break down this obstacle into small enough chunks she knew it was surmountable. Anything overwhelming or massive in scale was achievable when you knew the list of individual tasks required to get there.

The shipyards must be close to Earth. The cost would be mitigated and they would be more defensible. That was her starting point. But she could only see one side of the planet from here, and a probe that got close enough would certainly be shot down. So what assets did she have on Earth? Nothing. Only a single remaining agent of the Doc's, a wily woman whose sole job seemed to be as a quasi-celebrity net-presence. *Of course!* She was baffled by her own nearsightedness sometimes. The repeater was important because it was the only communication link, but for security she had been using it unidirectionally: to get people on Earth sympathetic enough to join her cause. Now that she had commandeered two engines of war all civilian space traffic was suspended. What remained was information gathering and trying to contact the Initiates on the ground.

She could get the net to work for her. With prods and pokes in the right places — hints and suggestions and leading questions on obscure forums, the darknet, the occasional social media post — she could convince amateur astronomers to search of their own free will. Effectively crowd-sourcing the hunt for the shipyards to the people of Earth, who could combine their points of view to see outward in every direction at once. Nothing in orbit could stay hidden from those paranoid, conspiracy-theory-loving legions for long. She could create an all-seeing eye, simply through online information manipulation. It would take time, so much time that it probably wouldn't help before the next wave of Earth ships were constructed, but she was confident she would survive that encounter. *Somehow.*

In the meantime there were other preparations to make. She doubled down on activity at the repeater. She knew that Earth-based telescopes could see it quite clearly, and that they would know exactly where to look. From an energy perspective, the L4 and L5 Lagrange points were the only two places it made sense to put a repeater to get around the sun's enormous electromagnetic interference. So if they looked at one and found nothing, they knew she would be at the other. It was therefore pointless to hide.

The advantage she *did* have is that relative to Earth they were always at the same angle. So she could present them a two dimensional facade and they would have no way of knowing what was behind it. Unless…unless there were a probe already to their side or beyond. Well, up until this point the vast majority of vessels in space were civilian, their paths public and well-documented. She could account for them. But she would also put some people on a new project to find any small, human-made craft not in Earth's vicinity. Scanning for metallic, regularly shaped objects should be easy enough with modern image processing power.

Knowing that she couldn't hide the repeater's location, but that she *could* distort its perception was a form of power. It was a potential threat the Harbinger intended to make full use of. A surprise ready for the heat of battle.

What to do with that potential was another matter. Grasping for inspiration, she pulled up scans on her pad of the surrounding area. Out here there wasn't much except for the asteroids themselves. They could be mined and refined, but all the purest minerals in the belt wouldn't matter one iota in the middle of a fight between behemoths. Unrefined, the asteroids themselves were a minor hazard at best, lazily orbiting the sun in predictable patterns. And even if she did attach thrusters to reposition a few they would still be seen well ahead of time and therefore remain easily avoidable. The asteroids would only be a threat if they magically appeared out of nowhere without warning…

She knew just enough physics to pull it off. Her education had never been more valuable in her entire life. It would be the fulcrum of her victory.

She made a note to send her battleships on one more towing mission each, to bring back two more of the stations the Renegade had thankfully cleared out, unknowingly helping her.

The Harbinger had turned her self-loathing about the Ace into a passionate need for vengeance so intense it was lustful. At first she thought it impossible to achieve, but thanks to this new plan her ingenuity had been revitalized. She would make use of what was available to her, however limited, and the result would be a thing of terrible, violent beauty.

Chapter 47: The Lion

The Lion was tense. Ready and waiting she held perpetually, perfectly still, about to pounce for days, then weeks on end.

She expected a swift and sure battering ram of a response, a giant god's hammer swinging down out of the sky to smite her.

But it never came.

Eventually she had to concede victory. It was a distinctly odd feeling. The Detroit Police Department never sent a second SWAT team. Given the state of the city, maybe they didn't *have* a second SWAT team. Or maybe they couldn't risk another loss like the one they had sustained, barely holding on to their limited control of the city as it was. So why not call in the National Guard? Would it have been too obvious? A flashing signal to looters and criminals that the city was there for the taking? Or were they trying to save political face, too embarrassed to admit they needed help?

Whatever the reason, after no activity for so long, nothing on the news or net, she allowed herself to loosen the tight kinks and knots bunching up her shoulders, and began planning for the future.

Without an immediate incoming threat, she felt comfortable leaving the compound again. She could recruit more. Find other cells. Maybe even go back to school. There was so much to learn and she realized that knowing how to manage people, keep accounts, or understand how solar panels worked were hard skills she was stumbling into without guidance. She yearned for knowledge in a way she never had before. Subjects she'd never shown interest in — business and math and finance and engineering — dominated her curiosity because for the first time in her life she desperately needed to know them. Knowledge wasn't an esoteric, abstract concept anymore. Knowledge was survival.

And they still had the captured police vehicles hidden nearby. With those she could go places she never had access to before. They were almost magical in their power, skeleton keys of transportation simply waiting to be used.

Was there anywhere *specific* she wanted to go before but hadn't dared? Somewhere she could make a difference? *That's my whole life, boiled down to a single question.* Now she had the first part of an answer, but wanted more, to expand her sphere of influence.

Strolling along the perimeter of the roof, looking out at the crepuscular city, it hit her like a brick. From the moment this had all started there were strong, tiresome rumors of a blacksite, somewhere they took bodies for examination and made permanent prisoners of the Initiates for interrogation. A pit of torture, death, and despair.

The Princess was cremated, but were those really her ashes? Could the Lion recover what was lost?

Dealing an unexpected blow to the authorities and adding to her own numbers at the same time sounded like a pipe dream. It was a Holy Grail of an operation. But now she had combat veterans, uniforms, police cars — everything she needed to pull it off.

And thanks to all the info online — the out of focus phone pictures taken from too far away, the leaks from officials who weren't entirely ethically sure of what they were doing — she knew where to look.

Thus a plan started forming in her mind, a rough chunk of wet clay already spinning into shape.

We're going to Chicago.

Chapter 48: The Renegade

He had expected more.

As the shuttle approached the asteroid, the Renegade was wary, his senses stretched until they almost snapped. He navigated with excruciating care, anticipating mines in the form of horrible little booby traps, like an explosive strapped to a small rock, innocent, floating aimlessly, doing nothing but waiting for him to trip its proximity sensor and blast the shuttle apart.

But so far, nothing.

And the nothingness gnawed at him.

The buildup occurring at the Lagrange point meant the Infected were serious about protecting themselves, but it looked like they were committing everything they had to that one location. In total, three stations had been towed there — one acting as a new repeater, the other two flanking it — and the Renegade let out a silent thank you to the universe that he had scoured those stations for supplies and personnel before the Doc's lost children got there. The Infected had also somehow acquired two massive battleships in their first clash with the forces of Earth. The area around the second repeater was growing increasingly dangerous.

Despite that, a second fleet, five ships strong, had launched and was headed with all haste to meet the Infected. Looking at the map, it was obvious a clash between titans was imminent. The Renegade didn't know if it would be decisive for either side, but all his wishes went with the vectors tracing back to Earth.

He concluded that, having left this asteroid utterly defenseless, they considered it of little strategic value, a non-military target. It was their living quarters, their home. You didn't keep watch or rig traps in your own backyard. Wars were fought far away on a foreign front somewhere.

All this time in space hadn't fundamentally changed how they thought. They trusted that conventions were followed. Mercy shown. They felt safe here.

They should have been paranoid.

While the shuttle slowed and used maneuvering thrusters to match the asteroid's wobbly spin, the Renegade watched several small blips slipping inside the rock. It gave him a good idea where the entrance was.

He thought maybe a few of them would stay outside to fight from the exterior. He wasn't sure how he would've responded to that. It was something no one had worried about before now. He knew that most firearms would kick enough to send someone careening off into space, tumbling for eternity. So he'd need something like a recoilless rifle. They'd be expensive to acquire, though perhaps not prohibitively so. Lasers and other radiation-based weaponry didn't fire projectiles and thus wouldn't have the same problem, but they did require huge power sources, impractical to be carried around by an individual. But maybe they could be mounted and connected to an interior power source, or even attached with cables for extra mobility.

His brain wandered back from the academic exercise of thinking about microgravity warfare. It was a moot point, for now. The Infected huddled inside their hollowed out rock. Cavemen afraid of a storm.

They were probably preparing for him right this second, assuming he would follow his usual pattern of docking and leading a force of boots on the ground. Creating an ambush, getting ready to pounce on him in the dark like they had on the first repeater. And this time they had a maze of freshly dug tunnels to their advantage, with no blueprints, no maps to guide him.

He bucked all the patterns of his past behavior.

The shuttle didn't land at the sole airlock. Instead, it parked a few hundred meters away. The Renegade and his small crew, already suited up, depressurized the cabin, opened the main door, and lugged their bulky cargo onto the surface. It was a heavy ordinance mining device, meant for blasting apart solid stone to get at the valuable minerals deeper down, or simply break up a large specimen into pieces of a more manageable size.

They angled it slightly inward toward the airlock, armed it, and boarded the shuttle again.

They repeated the procedure five more times, creating a rough hexagon on the surface, centered around the airlock. Following where the bombs were pointing resulted in a deep cone with a single intersecting point near the center of the asteroid. The Renegade was hoping that the ant-farm system carved into the rock didn't extend farther than that. If it did, he might have to put his musings about infantry space combat into practice.

On board the shuttle again, they finally repressurized the cabin and removed their helmets. As soon as they were clear of the estimated blast radius the Renegade unceremoniously tapped the final icon in the detonate sequence.

A rapid series of silent orange flashes blossomed brightly, drowning out all else. No sound or shockwave reached them through the void.

When the light died, he could see that the munitions had done their work better than expected: much of the asteroid near the bomb sites had been vaporized, the remaining chunks split in regular formations where hallways and rooms had been hollowed out.

"Search for signs of life. Any movement?"

"Sir...there," one of his crew said too slowly, words heavy in his mouth as he pointed to a display that showed a tight zoom in the visual spectrum.

The Renegade watched as a flailing body, unable to propel itself, but obviously still alive based on its motion, emerged from the shadow of the asteroid into direct sunlight.

The skin smoldered and burnt to a crisp in seconds. Blackened chunks of flesh broke away, brittle and flaky, like a log sitting too long in a fire turned to ash.

It didn't make sense, the project was supposed to harness the power of the sun, not turn people to dust when a ray hit them. The Renegade had assumed it was a success. That the Doc had gotten it to work ahead of schedule. Obviously that wasn't the case. He now remembered the curiously shuttered portholes on the repeater station, not letting a single crack of light through.

So where did the Infected get their energy? How did they sustain themselves?

"Are they all like that?" The Renegade asked through a gulp of doubt.

"About two-thirds as far as I can tell, maybe more," responded the crew member scanning the readouts.

So there had been normal, uninfected people in that asteroid. *Why? Why not infect everyone?* The Renegade began to sweat. He had killed potentially innocent people. But something else, a tingling feeling at the base of his skull he couldn't ignore, bothered him even more.

"Show me one of the others."

The display switched to show an unmoving corpse in the sunlight.

"Closer."

The camera zoomed in to reveal distinguishing features. A woman, blond, gashes and scrapes from explosive decompression evident.

A scarlet gouge on her neck caught his attention. It was almost circular. Not much deeper than the skin. The sort of wound an explosion didn't cause, and therefore must've happened earlier.

In a headache-inducing rush of memories the Renegade recalled the myriad clues. The strangely sharp teeth on the Infected at the repeater station. The pictures from the autopsy report the Investigators gave him. The jagged lacerations on his Husband's neck, roughly the same size and shape and location as the dark blood on this woman. The pieces of the puzzle waiting patiently for him to put them together. *Homo sum humani a me nihil alienum puto.*

What was it one of the Investigators had said? What did the wound look like?

A bite mark.

Chapter 49: The Captain

The distance to the Lagrange point and the new repeater station within it was rapidly diminishing. The Captain did a final fleet-wide status check for the umpteenth time, worried as he was about potential sabotage, mutinies, and whatever else the enemy had in store.

So far, all the status indicators were a familiar glowing emerald. This second fleet was still flagged by himself and the US-manned *Jackson*. The other member countries had invoked their naming rights once again and christened each of the new ships accordingly, sending out the *Daoguang*, the *Ahmed*, and the *Elphinstone*. The shipyards were configured to make four ships at once, so the *Pessoa* was a late entry by the youngest up and coming superpower, Brazil.

Five warships to take down two others and a defenseless station. The Captain had a creeping feeling that it was almost too easy, but that voice of caution could not contain his excitement. He had already come out of one battle unscathed, and was much better prepared for the second round.

It was in these calm-before-the-storm moments preceding combat when he waxed the most poetical. *And all the gods go with you! Upon your sword sit laurel victory!*

The approach vectors shrank and shrank and shrank until his flying-V formation was close enough that the scopes could provide a decent resolution in the visual range. Things were exactly like they had seen from Earth: the single sprawling station in the middle, acting as a makeshift repeater in the wake of the destruction of the first, flanked by a single compartment pod from other stations to each side. They hadn't been able to tell what had been done with all the other pods of those stations, only that they had been detached and moved, possibly dismantled for parts. The two enemy battleships were each flying a different pattern in a patrol around the repeater, one moving at an insane velocity that must have been built up over weeks of accelerating, the other slower and therefore more maneuverable, taking less time and space to turn.

Sure of his position and that of his foe, the Captain set about finishing what he started.

"Battle stations! Charge capacitors and arm all missiles! Target the —"

Two lines on his board instantly switched to bloody ruby coloring, and a screeching siren came on, demanding his immediate attention.

It was the status indicators for the *Daoguang* and the *Elphinstone* — the closest friendlies to him — showing a total loss of both the virgin vessels. *But the enemy ships haven't fired a shot.*

He pulled up outside cameras to confirm, not trusting the recently updated reporting software.

There, where each ship should be, was a cloud of debris, still traveling in parallel to the *Jackson*, matching its velocity. It was a haze of matter, organic and synthetic alike, reduced to harmless pulp. Those trillion dollar investments had been instantly pulverized.

The Captain's confidence had turned to shock and was quickly swinging into worry. *What could do this?*

He frantically rewound the external feeds, and what he found was terrifying: a *mass* the size of a house bowling through the length of each ship, almost perfectly aligned to their fuselages, moving far too fast for the framerate to accurately capture.

The ships had shrugged themselves apart, effortlessly making way for the unknown object.

Tracing the trajectories back led him to their source: the two station pods on either side of the new repeater.

In a horrible moment of realization, the Captain knew what the Infected had done. Earth didn't have a radar capable of penetrating the pods from millions of miles away, so he had only been able to guess at their purpose. He wasted precious seconds on a ping, waiting for its return across the deep, his mind frayed, unable to process whatever the bridge crew was shouting at him.

The results came back and he saw what he feared: the secondary stations had indeed been dismantled, piece by piece, and then reassembled into a single horizontal row of pods, stretching out in a manner that no architect had ever intended, hollowed out into a massive barrel. And behind each, asteroids were tethered like a line of schoolchildren, even now being nudged forward, the closest carefully entering the rear of the structures.

Railguns.

They made railguns.

And they're using asteroids as ammo!

Less than a minute had passed since the start of the engagement, but he already knew he was screwed. The planning, the meetings, all that brainpower and they never accounted for this. *We started building emplaced defenses, why didn't we think they would?* He staggered at the thought. The consequences. The hubris.

His logical mind momentarily regained control: he still commanded three ships to their two. And if he could just get the fleet out of the line-of-fire of those mass accelerators there'd be no way they'd be able to strike again. The stations-turned-guns would have to use thrusters to rotate the whole barrel, and they couldn't track fast enough to be a threat.

Confidence minutely renewed, the Captain silenced the crew, "Shut up! Tell the *Ahmed* and the *Pessoa* that they have to evade! We need to move!"

The order was tight-beamed across space. As his ship started moving out of formation he expected the others to follow as soon as they received and understood.

Instead, the *Ahmed* opened fire.

A full enfilade barrage hit the *Pessoa's* broadside. Flying in close formation like they were, there was no time to intercept the missiles. Even automatic defenses could not react quickly enough. The *Pessoa* flew apart in a firework display of violence.

The Captain had managed to reduce the number of ships affected by an infiltrator down from 75% in the first fleet to 20% in the second. In a theory class or a simulation in war college it would've been good enough to warrant a celebration. Here, it meant he had lost. That lives he was responsible for were destroyed. He started mulling through the list of families, the funerals needed to accommodate what happened under his command.

He almost gave in to the depression completely. He knew he couldn't win. Couldn't escape. Not a single ship against three. But the shining hope that pulled him back to reality was that he might be able to prevent this from happening yet another time.

"Fire everything we have at the stations." The enemy ships would be able to protect themselves, to intercept whatever ordinance he threw their way. But they were hopefully still far enough out that they couldn't fully protect the railguns and the repeater.

"Sir?" Someone balked, not grasping the situation, thinking the ships the greater threats, still concerned for their own life. *A stupid, foolish thing to care about at this point.*

"Do it!" He screamed, raw and frenzied.

Hard radiation banks spewed out actinic beams to incinerate the two stations that had been bastardized into cannons. Their components melted and fused into each other. Missiles whipped out to impact what was left.

The repeater's forward face had some sort of extra shielding. *Maybe taken off the ships they captured?* It withstood the fusion-powered lasers, and the missiles headed for it were destroyed in flight by the orbiting enemy ships.

The Captain knew he didn't have time for a second pass. The *Ahmed* was reloading its missiles, recharging its capacitors, and would have a firing solution in seconds.

"Take us straight up the middle into the remaining station."

The bridge crew looked around at each other, at him. Some scared, some bewildered. But seeing his stern resolve steadied them. The ship changed course a fraction of a degree.

The *Jackson* pointed directly at the repeater.

Impact warnings lit up and klaxons blared in his eardrums.

The enemy tried to stop him. *Lasers and masers and missiles, oh my.* But with this much mass it didn't matter if the ship was intact or functioning when it collided with the repeater.

The Captain stood to meet his doom and raised a one finger salute to greet his foes.

Chapter 50: The Lion and the Cub

The four-story, red-brick building with frosted windows started life as a warehouse. It fell into disuse when riots over civil rights made the poor part of town it was in even poorer. And, when the pricing hit rock bottom, the government acquired it.

Homan Square was notorious in Chicago for being a place one didn't go. Because of the rumors of the extreme torture happening inside even the criminal element stayed away. The streets were deserted. The nearby buildings rotting in disrepair.

The Cub was driving, and had stopped the co-opted SWAT van a block away for observation.

After a last breath to steel her nerves, the Lion nodded, signaling the go-ahead.

As they approached the gate to the small, fenced-in parking lot, the Lion wondered at how a place could go from holding consumer goods to holding the consumers themselves. This was the epitome of the behavior and lack of regard for life that had gotten the Princess killed. The rights being violated here in the name of safety and protection added fuel to the internal fire of her rage. But it was a cold fire, something not to consume her, but instead a source to draw energy and concentration from in these first, most vital moments.

The single occupant of a cramped guardhouse at the gate saw the police markings on their vehicles and waved them through. It was all the proof she needed that social manipulation of expectations was the easiest way to compromise security systems.

After parking, the Cub stayed behind with the van, ready for a quick getaway if the first part of the plan failed.

The Lion took the lead. She was clad in a hastily tailored police uniform, her hands on an Initiate who had been loosely handcuffed. She led him through the outer door, which was unlocked, while the rest of her team — Initiates all, some uniformed, others similarly restrained — followed. Inside, a desk protected by fiberglass housed a bored looking corrections officer entranced by a sudoku page in the back of a magazine.

The Lion coughed to get her attention.

The officer looked up. "Haven't seen you before. Just started?"

The Lion had prepared for this and every eventuality she could think of. "Yeah, took them forever to finally grant my clearance. It was worth the wait. First day on the job and we hooked a couple big ones." She indicated the handcuffed Initiate.

The officer grunted. "I'll get someone down here to take them off your hands. Nice catch."

She typed a few commands into a console, and a moment later a guard in full riot gear approached the first set of airlock-style bars farther down the hallway. The officer at the desk entered a few more commands and a gate in the bars opened, allowing the guard to pass through. When it had closed again the second, near gate opened and he approached.

After giving the Initiate a once-over he quipped, "Why didn't you tranq or tase them?"

The Lion panicked. *Of course* they would want their subjects subdued until they were properly restrained. She played into her earlier role: "Sorry, it's my first day."

The guard stared at her for a long moment, but then motioned for the Initiates to enter through the gate and stand in the barred area. "Huh. When I'm done dropping them off you'll have to tell me how a little girl managed to round up such big fellas."

She put on her best oblivious smile over gritted teeth. "I'll be here."

The desk officer entered a few more keystrokes and the nearest gate began closing.

That was the moment they were all waiting for. Now the commands to open the path in both directions were in the recent history of the terminal. They wouldn't have to spend valuable time digging through the system trying to find them.

The Lion nodded to one of the uniformed Initiates near her. He stepped up to the fiberglass window and with a spiked-brass-knuckles-fist punched straight through it. The officer shrieked and shoved her rolling chair back from the glass. The glass didn't shatter, so the Initiate punched a few more times in a rough circle, so that a big chunk fell away and he was able to climb through. The officer was fully screaming at him now, her back against the wall. He punched through her skull into the sheet rock behind and the noise stopped.

Meanwhile the Initiates with the guard inside the gates slipped out of their cuffs and attacked him all at once. He went down gurgling on his own blood while they fed.

The Initiate inside the booth opened the gate for the rest of them and the Lion led the pack through. When the second gate finally opened and she stood on the other side she let out a sigh of relief.

The hardest, most critical phase was complete.

Risk abated, the Cub entered, and swapped places with the Initiate at the front desk, face full of concentration. She set to work on the terminal while everyone else moved on.

Attacking at night meant there was only a skeleton crew of guards. The Lion had correctly assumed that the torturers and executioners of this place would believe they were committing all these crimes for the greater good, and thus hold to standard business hours like everyone else. Standing amid the masses on the subway platform pretending they had a normal job.

It made things much easier. The midnight shift meant the guards who were here were at the bottom of the pecking order, unable to secure a daytime position. They'd be tired since their circadian rhythms were out of whack and they were most likely bored to the point of sleep even if they were well-rested.

The Lion's group finally emerged from the short hallway into the center of the warehouse. Here a vast, open room held dozens of cages grouped together in the center of the floor. It stank of unwashed flesh and people forced to live in cells without plumbing. There was also something fouler in the air, perhaps burnt hair or decaying intestines. She couldn't tell, but it was probably the result of an advanced interrogation technique.

Along the perimeter of the ground floor were makeshift rooms of temporary walls that inevitably held instruments of pain. Modern racks and wheels and iron maidens updated for a new century, backed by funding from taxpayers' dollars.

Interlocking levels of catwalks overlooked the mayhem, patrolled by two pairs of guards. The Lion had worried they would hear all the noise from the front desk, but now realized that screams must've been commonplace here.

With quick, pointing motions she ordered her Initiates to take out the patrols. They clambered up the sides of the walls and catwalks unbelievably fast. Then their human-shaped blurs raced along the grating and attacked. One of them simply snapped a guard's neck. Another bit through some of the armor to pierce the jugular, blood raining down on the cages below as it sprayed from the wound. One guard went down with a caved-in face, and the last flailed his arms silently as he fell before crunching into pieces upon impact.

It was swift and quiet and over already. The Lion was continually amazed when she saw the power of the Initiates unleashed. And sometimes jealous. But what awed her the most was that even with their raw strength they chose to follow someone like her. It was simultaneously humbling and inspiring.

She sent the Initiates into the side rooms, but didn't bother to check who or what they found there. She trusted them to take care of it.

The deceased guards had keys that turned the huge steel bolts on the cages. She saw the hope of rescue in the eyes of every person inside. Most looked thin and jaundiced, starved and beaten. She didn't have to say anything, but she did anyway.

"We're getting you out of here. We have a place where you'll be safe."

The Initiates unlocked all the cages and supported or carried those who couldn't stand by themselves. They ushered everyone to the front and through the gates in several waves. She was the last one out, taking a long look at what they left behind.

She considered torching the place. It would've sent a nice message.

But after much contemplation, mapping all her actions to roads and following each to the end to see where it led, she opted for a subtler plan. When the Lion at last passed through the final gate, free once more, she looked to the control desk through the hole in the glass. The Cub was still there, finishing the masterstroke.

She had deleted all the security footage she could find, removing their faces and therefore masking their identities. And she had copied all the logs and data available. It might not have anything useful, but if an official had visited they might find a new target buried in the bytes.

Or, the Lion allowed herself to hope, *lists of prisoners, and hidden among them a Princess, alive and unburnt.*

The final piece was a virus that would continue to send them copies of anything new on the local system, and also suss out the network connections this facility had. If it worked it might eventually map out other compounds for them to hit. Or let them know exactly where the funding was coming from. It was a stepping stone to larger operations.

Plans within plans. It was diabolical. A word the Lion found she liked applying to herself.

When the Cub had wiped the last traces of their intrusion a minute later, she joined the Lion and the two of them exited the facility without a word. Neither of them wanted to jinx the operation.

Everyone they rescued had already piled into the back of the SWAT van. The Cub and the Lion joined them, hopping into their seats up front. Sporting a grin, the Cub started the engine and drove steadily up to the gate barring them from the street.

The guard was more interested this time. The Lion rolled down the window to talk to him.

"Did I see you loading up a bunch of detainees? Where are you taking them? We don't have a transfer scheduled."

"Oh, sorry I didn't tell you," the Lion replied nonchalantly. "We're freeing them."

The guard's face took on a look of confused disbelief, like he couldn't decide if she were telling the truth or testing to see how gullible he was. The look quickly morphed into shock and then horror as an Initiate reached across the Lion and yanked the guard through the window, tossing him back into the mass of newly freed ex-prisoners.

They were *hungry.*

Chapter 51: The Major General and the Orderly

"Disaster!" The Major General was shaking his head, standing over his desk and yelling at nothing in particular. The Orderly was sitting across from him, ready to take notes on her pad, but he wasn't saying anything she felt appropriate to write down.

"This is a disaster!" He was repeating himself now. Obsessing over the loss. The Captain. The good men and women, irreplaceable. He might not be able to find their like again, willing to sacrifice themselves against a foe they didn't yet understand. And those graceful, brutally destructive machines, now being used against their creators...

The Orderly decided to prompt him for some action items she *could* write down: "Sir, I know things didn't turn out like you hoped. But what do you think we can do about it?"

He looked a bit startled, like he hadn't realized she was in the same room, watching him throw his tantrum.

"We can't do anything. We needed a win to keep the shipyards rolling. A sign that this was all worth it. We didn't get that, so we have to shut them down. Kill the power. Send everyone home."

She started writing.

"But not a full decommissioning! We'll let them rest while we work on the political situation."

He finally sat down and continued, "We have to keep the defensive battery array active. They'll see that. They must."

"It's finished then?"

"Barely. We've got full coverage, but it's stretched to the max. If even one satellite gets knocked out there'll be gaps. They aren't manned, so they cost almost nothing to run. We need more though. We can't rely on them all working forever, even if they don't get wiped out during an attack. And with the repeater down we can't track those ships on the far side of the sun. Was it worth it to knock out their communications when it meant also gouging out our own eyes? We'll have to make probes to monitor them. Yet another expense. Right when we need budget the most is when they're taking it away. If the enemy knew how weak we were they'd be here at our doorstep, striking right this moment."

"It's a good thing they don't know our situation then. They'll think we're preparing another fleet. They'll wait to see what we throw at them." She was trying to cheer him up.

"True, we can use the extra time to our advantage. And there's a press conference scheduled to tell the public the space-based threat has been eliminated, so we have time to maneuver down here as well." His grim countenance slipped, brightening a shade or two.

He caught himself; prevented his own mood from lifting. The Major General had to be serious right now, had to be concerned.

He was responsible for doing all the worrying for all of humanity.

Virtually no one knew how much danger they were in, how close they had come to a global epidemic. And those who did were no longer willing to pay the financial cost to ensure its prevention. Keeping the Infected out of Earth's atmosphere had proven to be the most expensive venture in human history. The power brokers were probably too far removed, and thus felt too safe, to care now. They had other concerns like earnings reports to worry about. And there was that new domestic terrorist group that slaughtered the compound in Chicago. There were always a lot of distractions on the ground. That's why it was his job to look up.

Luckily before it all fell apart he had finally finished getting a full quarantine in place, now backed up by the weaponized satellite array in orbit, but it was a fragile, brittle thing. One accidental bump and the vase would teeter off the edge, shattering into a thousand pieces.

"We'll use every last second we can," the Major General declared. "Nobody knows the first shots in the fight for the future have already been exchanged."

He rubbed at tired eyes. He hadn't slept much, knew he wasn't going to sleep more anytime soon. Knew he had already pulled in every favor owed. He wasn't sure anyone would take him seriously now that he had twice lost entire fleets to the enemy.

"And the war has only just begun."

Chapter 52: The Harbinger

She had escaped the calamity of her people.

Again.

Have I always been this lucky?

The Harbinger was sitting on the bridge of the *Edward Teach,* with the *Ching Shih* and the newly renamed *Oruç Reis* nearby. The Captain's sacrifice had turned her brilliant plan for defending the repeater into nothing but silent desolation. So the three ships turned toward home.

As soon as communications ceased emanating from the asteroid habitat they endured impossible g-forces to race ahead at full speed.

They arrived to ruin.

Fully a third of the rock was gone, crumbled to dust.

The Harbinger knew without having to be told that it was the same third that housed all of their hollowed out chambers. While they were preoccupied at the repeater, the Renegade had dealt a decisive, murderous blow.

She peered outward into the vastness of the universe, and inward, only to find the same abyss. It allowed her to let the sterile metal and plastic of the ship fade around her while she thought back to her childhood.

She *had* won at games of chance more often than not. She had attributed that to skill with numbers or an uncanny ability to read her opponents. But now that she thought about, perhaps it was dumb luck.

The past seemed to unfold and open to her in a kaleidoscope of possibilities. Could luck be another force in the universe, not yet understood by science? And was there a confluence of it around her? In her? Invisible fields of gravity and radio and magnetism swirled around everyone everyday and no one had a way to know it using human senses. Maybe luck was another fundamental aspect and she carried a localized concentration of it around with her. A rabbit's foot anchored to her soul.

The Harbinger shook her head. Coincidence explained her surviving while those close to her died. Certainly there were others who had been alongside her each time the Renegade or Earth's representatives slaughtered her people.

She desperately wanted, *needed* an explanation though. A part of her brain would not stop thinking about what made her so special, to be spared while others perished.

The Doc had ultimately been right: she didn't care about her original mission anymore. Back then she had been an Agent of someone else's will, blind to her own power of choice and self-destiny, numb to whether the larger plan for Japan ultimately succeeded or failed. She hadn't really cared about anything for most of her life, and now that she did it was unraveling before her. She was helpless to stop it, a bystander unable to participate despite repeated attempts, grasping at motes of dust in a sandstorm. Perhaps this was karmic torture, ensuring that once she had something, *someone* to care about, she would be forced to watch them be destroyed time and time again, her eyes not allowed to blink while witnessing the repeated carnage.

She knew she couldn't handle it happening again. Not this soon. She needed somewhere safe to recover. But nowhere was safe. The fleets of Earth would pursue her to the edge of the solar system eventually. They were slow moving in their preparations, but it was a steady relentlessness that kept them coming forever until the task was completed. Time mattered less for large bureaucratic institutions: they could afford to spend it. *And once a hound has the scent...*

Where to go?

It was a simple question that summed up her conundrum. Staring out into space, knowing what she was, the advantages of her people, and the collective mindset of Earth's billions led to only a single inescapable path: *There is nowhere to go. So we'll go nowhere.*

They had three working spaceships. The first of their kind, battle-tested and hardened against the worst of the void. They could live on the ships for many years. Go anywhere. See things no one had ever seen before with human eyes. A new kind of astronaut. To boldly go forth into the great unknown.

She said it out loud to the bridge crew as much as to herself: "This is our home now."

It might not work in the long run; components would fail, their food sources would age and die.

So it wasn't *the* answer to the question. But it was *an* answer. For now.

Chapter 53: The Lion and the Vixen

The Lion had survived her first hunt. She was inordinately proud of that. And proud of her team. She had insisted the entire building stop working and celebrate the victory. The previous night after they returned had been an orgy in the purest sense: revelry with drinks and drugs and whole rooms full of writhing bodies. This morning it was a headache-filled blur.

Using the Initiate's skills to their fullest potential — by way of organization and preparation — was the biggest difference she could see between her Enclave and everyone else. Those who got captured were alone or scared, thinking with the animal part of their brain. For her people, she was the focus of all that energy, a human crystal. Prismatic under pressure. *Diamond.*

She understood now — finally — her gift. The thing she could contribute, why she could lead: calculated, precise planning. And, as last night had proven, execution.

Despite the massive success, she still wanted more. She'd personally combed through all the stolen data, searching for even a hint of the Princess. There was no trace. She tried to convince herself that it was for the best. *Hold on to your vengeance, but leave hope behind.* The last vestige of a prior life, put to rest. Letting her move forward without any reservations, unburdened by the past. Confident. Cool. A stoic leader.

There were still moments when she didn't feel like she could maintain her composure.

This was one of them.

A strange woman had shown up at their door. Unannounced. Uninvited. And yet everyone seemed to be doing what she asked.

She had power, that much was clear. Whether it was from spells cast by her sultry voice or lures for her full figure fueled by fire-kissed hair, the Lion couldn't tell. Humans generally wanted to please attractive people. Maybe that's all there was to it. But this Vixen exuded confidence and leadership and for a moment it made the Lion feel like her old weak, pathetic self again.

She wasn't about to hand over the reigns. Not without a serious fight. She had built this place up from scratch. Commanded in bloody battle. This was *her* building, *her* Enclave. These were *her* people. The Lion knew that startup founders were often replaced by more experienced CEO's once the corporation grew sufficiently, and she couldn't let that happen here. Although this wasn't a business and their was no board of directors to make decisions, she knew that if the woman got enough support she could usurp the Lion's position, her most precious life's work.

So when they finally met it was in private. In the Dungeon. That office-turned-pleasure-palace, walls lined with toys and artifacts that would make some feel intimidated, others awkward, a few transfixed. A place the Lion was comfortable, and a setting she hoped would throw the Vixen off guard.

It didn't phase her.

"Who are you?" The Lion demanded, arms crossed, an angry hangover still biting at her brain.

"A...liaison. It's as simple as that."

"I find that hard to believe. You look like you're used to getting your way. Giving orders and having them followed without anyone realizing they've been told what to do."

The Vixen laughed politely. "Oh yes, there is some of that. I see now you feel threatened. Don't worry: I'm not here to take over, or give orders. Though maybe *suggestions* from time to time. I just felt that meeting in person would help build our relationship. Engender trust."

"Why would I trust you? I don't even know you. Or who you work for."

"I don't work for anyone. As I said, I'm a go-between. A facilitator. Someone who *is* used to getting her way, it's true, but also someone who gets things done."

"So why come here, to me?"

"Ah, now that is the first good question you've asked. You see, you've been working in consort with another faction, a group of people I care about, without even knowing it! You've furthered our interests and have been the most successful organization on the ground. Have you heard about the cults popping up throughout the Rust Belt? The raids on rural militias? Those were all groups like yours. As far as I know, they're all gone now, one way or another. The only survivors taken to Chicago, where you then miraculously rescued them! What you built here represents the single largest remaining population center of our kind. I have to say I'm impressed."

"So you represent other Initiates? More clubs started by people like the Veteran?"

"Not exactly. The Veteran was the start of everything here on Earth. All the other groups that formed came from him, including people who left before the police raid or simply weren't in the house at the time but never managed to find their way to you. And I was the one who *created* him. Which means your Initiates are all related to me. You could think of me as their grandmother, I suppose."

"You...you transformed the Veteran? Who did it to you? And what do you mean 'here on Earth?'" The Lion could not contain her surprise. She wasn't sure whether to trust this woman, but she *was* providing conclusions to lines of thought that had gone on forever, twisting in infinite Mobius strips of confusion, plaguing the back of the Lion's mind since this all began. Unknowable with the death of the Veteran.

"So many questions! Though you're the one person who's earned the answers. Very well. I was the first person the Doc came to after he acquired his powers. And he was the first person ever imbued with them. I'm assuming you've had trouble with some of your group trying to turn this into a cult or a church, trying to explain what's happening with mysticism or religion."

The Lion nodded. It *had* been an issue. One she stomped on whenever it reared its head.

The Vixen continued, "You're right that it's not, of course. Nothing supernatural about it. Though you may want to consider allowing the roots of a religion room to breathe and then control how it's shaped. Put yourself or someone you can easily control at the center. Create rituals that work for you, to enforce your own position. Humans predictably make up stories to explain things when they don't know the truth. It's a natural reaction. And some people are always going to prefer those stories, despite evidence to the contrary. The stories are more fantastic. More *fun* than hard science. And they make you feel special. Like you belong somewhere in this cold universe. The big religions all figured out how important that is long ago, which is why they've managed to stick around for thousands of years.

"But in our case the source is simple: it's a virus that modifies cellular DNA. It was developed in a lab by the Doc, originally meant to be used as a gene therapy to allow humans to survive in space, without air, and taking power from sunlight. Skin-based photosynthesis and respiration would allow us to move into space and build things more quickly, to ultimately start moving large portions of the population off this over-crowded planet."

The Lion almost couldn't contain her excitement: *All the facts are falling into place!* What this woman was saying made so much sense. It had the ring of *truth* to it.

And then she realized the sweet dream had been soured. The Initiates didn't take power from the sun. They burst into flames when it hit them full on, charring into a crisp so that their own movements broke their brittle bodies apart. But now she could see how that weakness might have formed: the lab had to first make human skin absorb sunlight at extremely high rates, *then* they could figure out how to convert that energy. "But the project wasn't finished. What happened?"

The Vixen grew serious. "One of the Doc's coworkers wasn't happy with what they were doing. He thought it would be misused. That they were creating a weapon. The Doc saw that it could be used that way, but rather than shutting down the project he used it on himself in its incomplete state, preempting any attempts to stop him. He saw the potential. He looked far into the future and knew that this technology was power, as much as gunpowder or nuclear bombs. And that its invention was just as inevitable. So he took charge of it, put the power in the only hands he knew he could trust completely: his own."

The Lion didn't even need to consider that. She knew it was true. The changes *were* power. And whatever the original intentions, power always came at a price.

Something else clicked into place: "The lab, doing this research, it must've been in space...and the Veteran, he was just returning."

"Indeed. I was the contingency plan, sent down by the Doc before a quarantine could be put into place. Seeing an opportunity, I empowered the Veteran along the way. A happy coincidence of timing. I didn't give the gift to anyone else because I didn't want my movements tracked. I am the free hand no one is watching.

"But now the Doc's legacy in space is threatened. In some ways they are much better poised to survive what's coming than you are. They're isolated and far away and it's expensive to fight them. But the governments of Earth and one of the Doc's former assistants have been attacking them anyway. They are seen as the bigger threat because they're loud and public on the net and in control of stolen resources and generally pissing off the Company by interrupting their work."

"All those videos online, from those people in space, they aren't a hoax?"

"No, they're very much real. Those people have been fighting battles, just like you. And like your activities, those events have largely gone unreported. But I'm here to change all that. I can communicate with them discretely. We can coordinate our efforts. They are fighting the same war, only the arena is different. And we have one huge advantage: I don't believe the authorities have figured out that your Initiates and the 'Infected' in space are the same. If they had, this building would be nothing but rubble."

The Lion realized there was an unspoken question: *Would she agree to help?* It made this crazy project of hers instantly bigger, grander. There was more at stake than she ever realized.

A part of her had known that she could slip away in the night. Find her way back to her parents' house in the suburbs. Re-enroll at school next semester. None of these people knew who she was. Not her true name. They wouldn't be able to find her.

She had been holding out. Not fully committing herself, even to those who risked their lives for her. It was unfair. She owed them. Owed the Princess her revenge.

"Yes," the Lion said, rooted and resolved. She felt a burden lift from her shoulders, taken away by unseen angel wings. That implicit decision, the question of her commitment, had been weighing her down and she hadn't even realized it. "I'll help them. Be their ally here on Earth."

"Good," the Vixen declared, their business concluded.

She abruptly took an obvious interest in the walls of the Dungeon, as if seeing them for the first time, full of suggestive objects and art. A playfully innocent expression appeared on her face. "Then, with that decided, can we use this place for its original intention? It looks like a lot more than a private meeting room."

At that, the Vixen skillfully shed her outer layers to reveal a diaphanous slip underneath.

The Lion was speechless. She had never been with someone so stunning. So voluptuous. Given her own bony physique, she'd always thought a woman like this was out of her league. Now that she knew it was about to happen…a devious smile came to her lips at the same time she felt a quiver between her thighs.

"We can," the Lion responded. Mischievous thoughts at what she could do with such a body were already running rampant. "But we do things my way."

Chapter 54: The Renegade

The Renegade stared out the window through the vast emptiness to take in the giant blue marble hanging there, rotating sluggishly, going about its day as it had for millions of years before humans started scurrying over its surface.

He wanted to stop and take a breath. To feel like he could return to his normal life. To being an Assistant. To get back planet-side and never leave *terra firma*. To lay down his gun and never pick one up again.

He felt as if he almost could. That he'd come to the very end of his mission, a shear black edge spanning from horizon to horizon, which he hadn't seen until a moment ago, but had been walking toward all the same these long months. And all he had to do was take one more step to abandon his crusade forever. To begin to forget this time.

But something held him back. Stayed that last step. Kept the breath from finally releasing and his lungs relaxing.

There was a nagging feeling that he had missed something. Someone. That although lives had been lost to exact his revenge in the name of protecting that spinning globe from this new threat, it wasn't enough. The vigil remained incomplete. The sacrifice insufficient.

A lieutenant of his entered, and upon seeing the contemplative look on the Renegade's face, simply stood next to him and also stared out the window.

The Renegade somehow knew this fight wasn't over, despite his victories. And the more he thought about it, the more he realized why. His adversaries were not supervillians created in a lab accident. They weren't Infected carriers of a disease. Weren't Initiates in a cult.

This was nothing less than an ancient myth rising out of the pages of history and manifesting in the present. And he had played a part in it. A part perhaps prophesied, perhaps inevitable, perhaps not.

He turned to look at his lieutenant, who returned his gaze with level eyes and nodded. As if his subconscious had worked out the details simultaneously, the jigsaw puzzle pieces — numerous fights with the beasts, knowing how they acted, their weaknesses, what they needed to survive — all finally locking firmly into place.

The Renegade hesitated. He didn't want to say what he was thinking out loud. As if uttering the words would give them meaning, make them real. But he was fundamentally a scientist. A truth seeker. And he couldn't abandon that now. Any fact he had was a possible weapon against the enemy. He couldn't deny himself that.

So he accepted the words. And breathing them out gave them life.

"They're not genetically engineered," he declared.

"They're vampires."

About the Author

Brendan is a serial entrepreneur with a degree in computer engineering from Olin College.

He lives in Chicago with his wife, Monica.

He writes when he can find the time.

This is his first novel.

You can find him online at http://www.bdoms.com

CPSIA information can be obtained
at www.ICGtesting.com
Printed in the USA
LVOW11*0518311016

510983LV00001B/1/P